We Are Not Alone

We Are Not Alone

Selected Tales of Terror

by

Caleb S

We Are Not Alone

Caleb S.

To my father, Daniel S., who single-handedly established my love for reading, writing, and horror. I forgive you for the nightmares from letting me watch scary movies long before I should have.

We Are Not Alone

Content

Rose	9
Chatty Cathy	13
We Are Not Alone	35
The Diggins	91
They Need Help	119
Every Day is the Same	163
Author's Note	197

Rose

Under the quarter moon, Rose led him by hand down the trail at Ransom Lake. It was a popular trail during the day, but so late at night on a Tuesday, they had it to themselves. He had worried about the heat and the bugs, but both had been tame.

This dream didn't come often, but when it did, he welcomed it with open arms. It was the first time they made love. He knew he was dreaming, the way you sometimes do. A blessed nostalgia filled him as he felt the warm June night air, smelled the sweet scent of pines, felt her hand in his, and saw her face, remembering it as if he hadn't gone the last too many years without seeing it. This was the only time he could let himself remember how she looked. Her wavy black hair, her enticing smile, her round eyes, her hundreds of freckles only just making their appearance for the season. He thought himself the most average a man could be. Average height, average looks, no discernable skill or talent. But Rose... Rose was everything. Every word she spoke to him was a blessing, every kiss a miracle to be savored.

"Over here," she whispered with a giggle of excitement. He followed her off the trail. He couldn't take his eyes off of her as she wandered through the brush, searching until she was satisfied with a flat place on the ground. They kissed, and despite his nerves, he felt himself growing erect. Rose noticed and touched him through his jeans. Their lips separated, and she kissed his neck. A gasp escaped his throat, and he found himself struggling to breathe or even stand. The anticipation was overwhelming him. He could smell her lotion and see her tan skin even in the dull light, wanting to touch every inch of it.

Finally, she gently guided him to the ground and slipped her dress above her head. He pushed his pants down past his knees and she mounted him. They both gasped as he entered her. She was wet and tight, her youthful body making him feel like he had never felt before. The moonlit sky behind her silhouetted her figure against the trees, her expressions of passion and noises of pleasure filling the air around them as she moved herself back and forth. Her breasts, perky and firm, perfect in size and shape, pushed together just in front of his face and he was already struggling not to finish. He closed his eyes, feeling her move against him and feeling the presence of a love that would only grow more with every day. The feeling, the setting, the time and place. It was all perfect. Until he opened his eyes.

It wasn't what usually happens. The dream always ended with the two lovers climaxing in unison, shouting out in pleasure and holding each other as they shook from the excitement. This time, something was wrong. She wasn't moving any more. The insects weren't chirping. The air no longer had that beautiful aroma of pine and earth. It reeked.

He opened his eyes to horror. Rose was on top of him, but her body was not what it had been when they were youthful, lusty lovers in the woods behind campus that he always dreamed of. It was the body that the police found on the bank of the Grand River six months after they'd gotten married. Her head was missing, her neck ending in a mess of blood and sinew. Her body was gray and bloated with decomposition. Open sores speckled her torso and leaked black puss onto his belly. Horrified, he scrambled out from under her. He stood but was frozen, unable to run. He wanted only to save her, but she was beyond that. Her body stayed in the position as if she still straddled him. Before his eyes, she began to rapidly decompose. Her body darkened, the skin began to fall away, the insects ate at her flesh.

He screamed, not from terror, but from grief. The body leaned back, exposing the severed stump to the sky. The blood that fueled her heart that beat only for him came out in trickles over her once immaculate breasts that were now indiscernible from the rest of the rot. She made no noise. But she was screaming, too.

Chatty Kathy

On a warm autumn night in Tennessee in 1987, it didn't have to be Halloween to find the town's youth out of the house worrying their parents and doing what teens do. But tonight *was* Halloween, and two particular couples were taking advantage of the unseasonable warmth of this October evening. It didn't come around that often in the town of Chester. A town that was more than "in the middle of nowhere", it practically *was* nowhere. There was a small restaurant, a small school, and a small post office. It was a place of boredom and a breeding ground for troubled teens. It was a dark town. A harvesting place of mystery and local legend.

Usually regarded as good children, our quartet was on what some of the older folks would call a "wild streak". They began the evening stealing candy from porches, ignoring signs that said, "For Kids Only", or "Please Take Only One!". They cruised the back roads of Chester in a 1984 Chevrolet Chevelle SS, who's real owner was the father of its driver. Tim's father would undoubtedly disapprove of his driving the car, but he was all the way in Memphis for a corporate party and, if you asked Tim, probably busy snorting coke out of a hooker's bush.

As if this wasn't enough, Tim had scored a box of smokes from his older brother, who didn't even charge him double for the trouble.

They were parked at the end of a cul de sac in their neighborhood. Two in front, two in back. Cigarette smoke billowed from the windows, accompanied by Van Halen's "Jump", which the entire neighborhood was listening to whether they liked it or not.

"Tim, this is great and all, but I have school tomorrow," Maddison whined as if they didn't *all* have school the next day. Tim groaned but made no reply. Maddison was such a buzzkill, but with a glance at her shorts in the rearview mirror, he could see why Tyler kept bringing her along.

"Come on, baby, it's only nine," Tyler said, "Don't be such a square." Maddison sighed and moved away from his attempt to kiss her, but the backseat of the Chevelle didn't give her much room and he ultimately planted one on her cheek.

Danielle, Tim's girlfriend, started to form her own complaint but didn't get a chance to finish. Tim had turned the radio to its maximum volume. He took another puff of his cigarette and turned his head to blow it out the window. Danielle seized her opportunity to punch the radio's power button, abruptly shutting off the music.

"Hey!" Tim screamed. "Don't touch my shit!" He turned the radio back on, just for Danielle to turn it off again. This cycled again, on and back off, before Tyler shouted from the backseat.

"Guys, cool it! This shit is giving me a headache. The music is too loud back here anyway, Tim. Give it a break, will you?" Tim rolled his eyes.

"That's adorable. Did she tell you to say that?" He pointed the rearview mirror toward Tyler, who shifted uncomfortably when their eyes met.

"No," he said simply. Tim snickered at him. Taking another drag, he said; "I don't believe you. We used to burn through these streets with music as loud as this without the girls in the car and you never had a problem."

"Yeah," Tyler admitted, "but I'm not in the backseat when we do that. These windows don't roll down back here, it's loud as fuck. Just lay off for a bit."

Tim didn't say anything else but left the radio off. Light wind whistled through the window as Tyler and Maddison began making out. One look at Danielle and he knew his chances of getting it in tonight were slim to none, which was all the same to him. He was used to not getting any action by now. He hadn't gotten off with her in three weeks, and even that was from an unenthusiastic hand job.

Although he couldn't help being a little jealous of Tyler right now.

Danielle was in sweats and Tim was convinced it was just to be a prude. They all knew it would be warm tonight. Tyler was dressed in an impressive Jason Vorhees costume, which fit his tall and muscular stature. Maddison complimented him in skimpy brown shorts and a revealing yellow t-shirt that read "Camp Counselor". Tim and Danielle picked them up from a Halloween party at Maddison's parents' house, to which they had not been invited, hence their lack of costumes.

Tim watched as Tyler cupped Maddison's breast, and his eyes shifted to Danielle. She instantly knew what his look implied and shook her head.

"Not here," she said under her breath. Tim responded with "Then where?".

"Not here!" was her final answer.

Tim shrugged dismissively and turned around. "You guys want to go somewhere?" he asked the two in the backseat. "I'm bored as hell."

"Bored as hell?" Tyler mocked. "You mean Danielle won't let you grab a titty in front of an audience? That sucks, dude. Maddison likes when people watch!" To prove his point, he squeezed Maddison's boob through her shirt.

"Ouch, jerk!" Maddison shouted. "And I do not!" She slapped him on the shoulder and crossed her arms over her chest. When Tim laughed at him, he received a similar slap from Danielle.

"Maddison, do you want to go?" Danielle offered. "I'll walk home with you and have my mom pick me up."

"Woah, woah, woah," Tim interjected. "Everyone hold their horses. Who said anything about going home? The night is still young, my friends!"

"Not if you keep treating us like objects," Maddison threatened. Tim thought of a funny joke to make, but he was starting to believe they may actually leave if he were to anger them any further, so he kept it to himself.

"Okay, fine. I'm sorry." Neither girl verbally accepted his apology, but neither made a move to escape the Chevelle either, and he believed that was just as good. Before the silence could become an *awkward* silence, Tim had an idea.

"Who wants to go check out the old Brady house?" He asked. Maddison and Danielle both groaned.

"What?" Tim asked, surprised. "It's just an old house!"

"Let's do something else, bro," said Tyler. Tim could hardly believe what he was hearing. He could understand the girls being upset, but Tyler? It didn't make sense. They'd talked about breaking into the old mansion on many occasions.

"Can't we just drive to the river and go skinny dipping or something?" Tyler asked, but it was not enough to appease Tim.

"Not unless you plan on filling up this gas tank. The river is like an hour from here! What's gotten into you, man? We've always wanted to go there!"

"Yeah, but…" Tyler searched for an excuse, then found one. "Yeah, but it's all boarded up in there, you can't even get in."

"Wrong," Tim disputed, "My brother has gone in there to drink before. He said there's a door around the back by the pool that's unlocked. That's how everyone else gets in there."

"Right," Tyler replied. He leaned forward to whisper in Tim's ear. "Look dude, it sounds fun, but the girls will get scared big time in there."

"We will not!" Maddison shouted, having not only heard the remark but been offended by it. Danielle looked at them with an offended expression of her own but had nothing to add.

"Alright then," Tim said, taking his chance. "Prove it. We'll go there right now and if you girls can last five minutes in a room together without us, we'll do whatever you want to do the rest of the night."

"You would do that anyway if you really wanted some ass." This came from Danielle, and

Maddison chimed in her support with "Yeah, girl! Tell him!"

"Come on," Tim nearly begged, "I'm serious. We've been sitting here on the side of the damn road for half an hour. You won't even let me listen to music. I just want to have a good time, man! It's Halloween and I want to be spooked by something other than Tyler's breath for a change. Let's go to the Brady house, get inside, look around, burn a couple of cigs, then we'll bounce. I know you guys want to see the inside of that place as much as I do. Everyone does."

Tim looked at Danielle, who looked at Tyler, who looked at Maddison, who shrugged and muttered something that didn't exactly sound like a rebuttal.

"Yes!" Tim exclaimed in victory, then started the car.

****

Tim parked the car along the side of the road a short walk away, fearing they were more likely to get caught if he were to park in the driveway. Nobody objected, as they were eager to escape the cramped conditions of the car, particularly those in the back seat. Finally out, Tim walked to the trunk and opened it, fishing around for the collection of tools his dad usually kept in there. He found a bag and produced two flashlights from inside, then handed one to Tyler before taking their first steps toward the house.

It was a looming, ominous structure in the night, its creepy nature amplified by the moonlight and more so by the vibe of Halloween night. It seemed to emanate a certain foreboding emotion, and none in the party of four approaching were without it.

They walked together in pairs across the length of the driveway and around the side of the house. Nobody said anything, but they all sensed the temperature dropping dramatically. It was enough to give Tim goosebumps, but he ignored them.

They walked along the back of the house, careful to walk only on the concrete and being as quiet as possible, though none of them could say why. Nobody even spoke until they reached the pool, and it was Tim who said the first words since getting out of his dad's car.

"There's the back door," he said, then pointed it out to the others. They huddled closer together as the wind picked up out of nowhere, and it was Tyler who gripped the handle of the door to pull it open.

The door opened without any form of resistance, and the group filed inside. Tyer shut the door behind them, cutting off what little source of light the moon gave them and plunging them into complete and unforgiving darkness.

"Okay, genius," Maddison said, nudging Tim, "We're inside. Now what?" He didn't answer right away, just flipped on his flashlight. Tyler did the same and between them, they could see most of the room they were in. Dust particles floated around them so thick, it was like standing in fog. The air inside smelled like mold and old books like Tim's father kept in his home office. They were in the rear of the foyer. Tim took the first steps into the house, and the others reluctantly followed close behind.

Finally reaching the front half of the house, everyone stopped when Tim shined his flashlight on the ceiling. Tyler's light followed and together, they focused on the crystal chandelier.

"Is that where-" Danielle began but was interrupted by Maddison. "Stop!" she shouted. "I don't want to hear about it." Danielle didn't need to finish her sentence, though. They were all thinking the same thing. They, along with every man, woman, and child in the county, had all heard the stories of Mr. Brady. A local musician and singing instructor who made the classic deal with the Devil to gain his talent and success. Nobody knew if that was true, but what everyone knew to be true was that he went crazy and killed six children. Two of his own, and four others who were students of his. He had lured them to his home under the guise of rehearsing for a new, very special performance. He carved out their eyes, cut their bodies open, and hung them from the chandelier - all to appease the Devil. He was found slumped against his grand piano beneath the bodies of those children.

"I thought you wouldn't get scared!" Tyler teased.

"Well, I am, so stop it." Maddison spat, and made it clear she was not in a mood to joke around. "Can we go? I'm getting sick to my stomach."

Tyler seemed about to give in, so Tim answered him. "No, not yet. We just got here! We have to at least look around first."

Without waiting for a response, he took Danielle by the hand and walked up the stairs. She followed and looked back to see Maddison still tugging on Tyler.

"Tim, I'm sorry but Maddison is freaking out." Tyler said. Maddison scoffed when he said this but didn't leave his side. "We're going to go back out to the car. Did you leave your keys in it?"

Tim wished he would have kept his keys on him, but he didn't. He told them the keys were still inside but not to touch anything. Maddison was relieved to hear this and was already dragging Tyler toward the back door.

Tim looked over his shoulder at Danielle and shrugged. She wasn't too happy either, he could tell. Ignoring this, Tim turned back toward the stairs and began ascending them. It took only a few seconds to reach the top. At the landing, Danielle let go of Tim's hand as they drifted apart. Tim walked straight toward the back wall, which housed a picture window looking out into the field behind the house. A reading nook was placed in front of the window, and he knelt on it to look out.

A commotion came from outside a moment later and when Tim and Danielle locked eyes, it confirmed they both heard whatever the noise was.

"It was probably just the car door. They better not fuck in my dad's Chevelle," Tim said then focused his attention back outside of the window. Danielle replaced her eyes in the hallway left of the stairs. She wanted to explore further but was not about to go into any of these rooms alone.

"Let's go in here," Danielle said, stepping in front of the door on the left side of the hallway.

"Well look who finally found her sense of adventure!" Tim said. He stepped off of the reading nook and met her where she stood. The door to the room was old and made of solid wood, he could tell. The knob was made of brass, and it was cold to the touch when he went to turn it. The door opened easily enough and revealed a room with a mess of toys on the floor. There was a bed against the wall with a broken headboard.

"I swear to God if you make some lame ass joke about 'breaking the bed even more'" she said this last part with air quotes, "I will leave you in here by yourself."

Tim, a little embarrassed because he was absolutely about to make a joke to that effect, said nothing.

They walked into the room side by side but parted once through the doorway. It was a big room with plenty of space for them to explore. Danielle felt a cool breeze and took note of an open window on her side of the room. She walked toward the dresser, which was topped with a vanity mirror and a few dusty pictures. She picked one up and wiped it off as best she could with the sleeve of her sweatshirt, but Tim had a flashlight and she didn't, so it was still too dark to make it out.

Across the room, Tim used the flashlight to watch where he stepped and also to illuminate the closet, where he found clothes that obviously used to belong to a young girl. Several dresses occupied the space, and they all looked like they hadn't been touched in years. Most had significant damage from what he could only imagine were moths or mice.

"I hurt myself!" screeched an ugly voice, shattering the silence they were just getting used to. Tim and Danielle both jumped and gasped at the sound then went to hold each other.

"What the hell was that?" Tim asked, failing to hide the fear in his voice. He scanned the room but saw nothing out of place.

"I think it was that" said Danielle as she pointed to a doll on the floor. It was a vintage pull string doll, about 20 inches tall with blonde hair and a blue dress. She hoped it was just the darkness in the room, but she was sure the doll had black eyes.

"An old Chatty Cathy? That thing is probably older than our parents, how could it possibly still work?"

It was a good question, and she couldn't answer it. Tim knelt to pick up the doll and held it in his hand.

"Do you think it belonged to the little girl that lived here?" Tim asked, "Mr. Brady's daughter?"

"No," Danielle responded, "I'm pretty sure these things didn't come out until the fifties or early sixties. I've heard stories about this, though. It's what people do. The little girl who lived here used to love dolls. So, to communicate with her spirit, people bring in these old pull-string dolls and use them kind of like a Ouija board. The legend says if you pull the string, it will be the ghost of Kara Brady that responds, not the doll."

"Sounds like a load of bull to me," Tim said, throwing the doll onto the floor. He got to his feet and was about to tell Danielle they'd better leave soon when the ugly voice of the doll spoke again.

"You shouldn't be in here," it said. Tim looked at his girlfriend, who shared the same puzzled look as he did.

"Is that one of its phrases?" Tim asked hopefully, but he could see in Danielle's face that she doubted it, and he did too.

"Wh-why not?" Tim asked the doll. No response came. "Why not?" he demanded. The doll said nothing, just laid motionless on the floor.

"Why are you trying to talk to it?" Danielle begged, "Let's get the fuck out of here! It's talking, for Christ's sake!"

"I just want to see what she has to say," Tim reasoned, "don't you? I've never talked to a ghost before."

"It won't talk unless you pull the string on the back," Danielle instructed, but Tim waved her away.

"We didn't have to before, did we?"

"No, but it isn't working now, is it? Maybe it only talked before because one of us stepped on it or something. I say we just leave it alone and go outside with Tyler and Maddi."

"Yeah, well I say we see what else little miss Kara has to say." He bent down and handled the doll again, turning it over and putting his index finger through the ring attached to the string in the doll's back.

"Why shouldn't we be in here?" Tim asked. With a gulp and the slightest bit of hesitation, he pulled the string, then let it go.

"He lives here with me," the doll responded eerily. The sound of a pen dropping could have been heard at that moment. The wind stopped blowing and the only sound was their own breathing.

"Who lives here with you?" He asked. His heart was pounding in his chest. He looked at Danielle, who had a tear streaking down her face.

She opened her mouth to say something when the doll, whose string had not been provoked, turned its head to look at them. Danielle screamed, and Tim looked back at the doll just in time to see its mouth move, accompanied by that shrill, hideous voice.

"The Devil! Ah-ha-ha!"

As if on cue, a crash came from downstairs. It was followed by Maddison's voice, screaming at them to come downstairs quickly.

Having no problem with that, Tim threw the doll at the floor a second time and was on his feet in an instant, grabbing Danielle by the arm and pulling her out the door of the bedroom. They were both screaming and panicking as they hit the staircase and hurried down.

"It's Tyler!" Maddison was screaming, though they hardly understood her. "We were walking back to see what was taking you guys so long and as soon as we got back to the property, he just started seizing up! I tried to help but there were all of these-these ugh… *shadows* everywhere, like - shadow people! I don't know, okay, but I was too scared to help him!"

When Tim and Danielle reached where she was standing, they blew past her and ran straight for the back door in which they had come in. Tim pulled the handle on the door, but it wouldn't open.

"What'd you do to this door, Maddi?" he asked, still jerking the handle. It didn't even budge despite all his effort.

"Nothing," she answered in a pipsqueak voice, "I just walked through it."

After another tug on the door, he gave up. "Son of a bitch!" he screamed and punched the glass in the door. It rattled but didn't break, and he saw no point in trying again. They were stuck in here.

Behind him, Danielle had found her way in the dark to the front door, but it too would not open. She was still trying when Maddison ran to her, wheezing. "What is going on?" she cried, "Why can't we get out?"

"There's a talking doll upstairs that just told us the Devil lives here!" Danielle explained to her in a hurry.

"My God," Maddison commented, "That's what Mr. Brady kept saying when they found him!"

"I know," Danielle screamed. She kicked the front door with all her strength. "How are we going to get out?"

"Have you tried any of the windows?" Maddison asked, then ran to the window nearest the front door and began pulling at it desperately.

Suddenly, Danielle remembered feeling the breeze from the open window in the room with the doll and was already running for the stairs before she yelled to the others.

"Tim, up here!" she hollered. "The window in that room was open! Here, follow me." She grabbed Maddison's arm and pulled her along as she went upstairs. By the time they got there, Tim was right behind them, and they were racing toward the bedroom to the left of the hallway. The door was open as they left it, and they hurried through. Tim was the last one in and slammed it shut behind him, then turned to lock it. The lock turned and when he tested the knob, the door didn't budge.

All three seemed to look in unison at the window that overlooked the driveway. The one that was opened earlier but is closed now.

"What's wrong?" Tim asked.

"It's not open anymore," Danielle replied with dread. Not sure what to do next, she put her hands in her face to cry. Maddison showed her support by hugging her and Tim hugged them both.

"Girls, girls," he said, trying to keep the fear from his voice, "It's okay. We just need to think of what to do next. That's all!"

"There is no next for you!" said a shrill voice that was familiar to all except Maddison, but she saw who it came from. They all screamed and scrambled away from Chatty Cathy, who was sitting upright on the floor in the middle of the room.

"He's coming! He's coming and you'll all die! You'll all die very, very soon! Aha-ha-ha!" Cathy was still cackling when the first knock came at the door. The three trespassers were still huddled by the window, screaming and crying when the second knock came. Soon, the knocking turned into pounding.

"No!" One of them cried. "Go away!" cried another. It didn't matter. Chatty Cathy was cackling loud enough to drown them out.

The next pound on the door caused it to bow inward and a splinter of wood shot from the door frame as it weakened.

"Only one story left to tell! The one where I send you all straight to Hell! Ah-ha-ha! Ha-ha-ha!" One last pound was all that it took to send the door flying open as the frame around the latch exploded into a thousand tiny splinters.

In the threshold was a dark mass of swirling black mist. All three trespassers could feel the raw evil emanating from it. The feeling of dread pouring from the entity was overwhelming to Maddison, who fainted. Tim and Danielle let her fall between them. Danielle began to plead, saying "Please, please, please," on a loop. Tim closed his eyes to pray desperately, but all attempts were to no avail.

"Open your eyes, fools!" Chatty Cathy instructed, "You won't want to miss this!" She spared them the giggling fit this time, but it did nothing to ease them.

When Tim opened his eyes. They immediately flooded with tears. Danielle tried to scream, but her voice had given out on her and she simply mimed the movements like a fish.

In front of them were six eyeless children, all stark naked and split open from groin to neck. Their bones were exposed, as well as their organs, which were spilling out as they walked toward them. Blood covered most of their exposed bodies, dripping from their fingertips as they reached toward each other and joined hands. When they formed a tight circle around the trespassers, their mouths opened in unison and a harmony was formed. As Chatty Cathy directed this choir of dead children, Tim, Danielle, and Maddison joined Tyler in being swallowed by the dark as their ears filled with a deafening song that no one alive has ever heard.

We Are Not Alone

The house on Turnbuckle Road came into view as Trent's Cadillac CTS crested a hill. It was a humble two-story home with large bay windows and a porch that ran the length of the front. It had been a long, bumpy ride since leaving the interstate nearly an hour ago, so the house was a welcome sight to Trent. His wife could not say the same.

"Oh my God," Emma said from the passenger seat. "Please don't tell me this is it. Please, Trent."

Trent didn't answer right away. He had expected this reaction. Emma was a city girl, born and raised in New York to a reasonably wealthy family that put her through college at Columbia University. She had rarely left the city on her own free will. She had never intended to, either. She'd never even owned a car.

Trent had driven the entire way to Georgia. Not that he minded. He loved to drive, though he didn't get to much since moving to New York. He'd played road games with Tommy until he'd fallen asleep in his car seat, then listened to an audiobook while Emma sulked and eventually slept with her headphones in. She woke up when they exited the interstate and hadn't spoken until just now.

"This is it," he said finally, then continued before his wife could complain further, "Tommy! Wake up, buddy, we're home!"

Emma looked as if she were about to vomit in her mouth. "Please don't say that." she muttered.

Tommy sat up in his car seat, extending his neck for a better look. "Woah!" he exclaimed. "That's our new house? The whole thing?" His son had spent his entire four years in a cramped New York City apartment and Trent feared Tommy would not grasp the concept of having a place of their own with land and things to do on it.

"It sure is, buddy," Trent replied. He stole a glance at Emma, who was staring intently through the windshield at the house, as if she was studying to find anything good to say about it.

They turned into the driveway and pulled up alongside a minivan with a sticker on it advertising a gray-haired woman named Rhonda as a realtor. She was standing on the porch with a briefcase, waiting for them to meet her.

Trent reached over and squeezed her hand. She was not expecting this and drew her hand back at his touch. She felt bad when she saw the hurt in his eyes.

"Just work with me here, Emma. We need this."

Except they didn't. If you asked her, they were perfectly fine in their apartment in the city, where there was always something to do or people to see within a few minutes' walk. The city's ambience lulled her to sleep every night and greeted her in the morning. They had the money to live practically anywhere in the city, but Trent chose to try and move them to the hillbilly country, and for what? A change? The "peace and quiet"? So that their son could grow up as some redneck, getting dirty and going to some no-budget public school? Trent thought the city would be bad for Tommy, but it turned out fine for Emma and practically everyone she knew.

Still, she thought there was a chance she could talk Trent into backing out of the deal. She would just have to act friendly with the realtor, make sure Trent didn't give her an answer right away, then plead with him to take them all back to the city to pretend the last 15 hours had never happened. She put on her "good wife" face, complete with a smile consisting of perfectly white teeth, and stepped out of the car.

"Hi!" Rhonda the realtor said, "You must be Emma!" She walked down the steps to meet the arrivals.

"That's me," Emma said politely. They exchanged pleasantries while Trent removed Tommy from the car seat. He joined them in front of the steps.

"Oh, Mr. Sinster, it is such a pleasure to meet you," Rhonda sang as she shook hands with Trent. "I am such a big fan of yours. I know it must be annoying hearing this, but would you care to sign my book?" She was already opening her briefcase to pull out a well-read paperback copy of Trent's debut novel, *Better Left to Fray*. Emma stared at the book, feeling something stir in her chest. It was at a book signing following this book's release that she met Trent for the first time. It was six years ago when he still lived in Denver, where he'd grown up, but had visited her university to promote the novel. The rights had just been sold to a movie producer and Trent Sinster was becoming a name of interest in the literary world. *Sign of the Times* and his preceding anthology titled *Us and the Night: Ten Thrilling Stories* had both earned a spot on the New York Times Bestseller list.

"I'd be happy to," Trent said, then took the book and an offered pen from Rhonda to sign. He handed the book back and watched her put it away.

"Thanks, Mr. Sinster. Now, are you ready to tour your new home?"

"Only if you call me Trent from now on," Trent said pleasantly.

Only if you never call it that again, Emma thought.

Trent told Rhonda they would follow her lead, and she brought them into the house. Emma had to admit, it looked better inside than she'd expected, but not by much. There was fresh paint and updated appliances, but it did little to hide the age of the home. It smelled of wood and earth and reminded her of a museum she'd visited in grade school. There was furniture that was covered in plastic and looked like it was purchased by someone's grandmother. The windows all had a blurry film of condensation on them despite it being dry and hot. She'd never felt Georgia heat before and was not impressed by it.

"The house was built in 1920 by-"

"1918, actually," Trent interrupted. "Oh," Rhonda said, looking down at her notes. Trent cleared his throat, "at least that's what I thought I read on the listing. Sorry to interrupt."

"It's quite alright," Rhonda said, looking up from her papers. "And you're absolutely right. 1918. There have been several renovations, of course...."

Emma tuned her out, staring down at her feet to keep her eyes from wandering. She didn't want to see the crack in the ceiling or the spiderwebs in the corner that she imagined were there. She would just keep her eyes on her feet, which didn't help much either because the floor was dull and peeling. She considered going back out to the car but decided against it. Sweating and staring at the house would do her no good, either.

They walked from the living room to the kitchen as Rhonda talked. Tommy seemed to be having fun running around from room to room. She did like the idea of having room for him to play, especially outside, but this wasn't worth it. There were parks in the city for that very reason.

They walked through a utility room and a separate dining area downstairs, then went upstairs, where there were three large bedrooms, two of which were on one side of the staircase, and one was on the other next to a second bathroom. The upstairs was worse than the downstairs. It felt like it was twenty degrees hotter, and everything had a layer of dust on it an inch thick. She was *disgusted*. The master bedroom was awful. It looked like something out of a horror movie. There was only one small closet and there was a queen-sized bed between two large windows overlooking the backyard. Just outside the window was the roof that overhangs the back porch. She imagined it would be easy for intruders to climb up and into the bedroom! What would stop them? Their apartment in New York had security around the clock, not to mention it was on the top floor of the building where there was no chance of a robber or rapist climbing a measly few feet onto their roof and letting himself in.

She prayed Trent was feeling the same way about the house, but when she looked at his face, her heart dropped. He had the biggest smile she had seen since their wedding day. He was loving every bit of it, and she found herself not looking forward to the conversation they would have when Rhonda left them.

Except when they rendezvoused back downstairs, Rhonda simply handed the keys and paperwork to Trent, told them to enjoy themselves, and left.

"What was that?" Emma asked. Trent didn't respond but had a guilty look upon his face. "Trent," Emma said firmly, "Why did she leave you the keys? Aren't we supposed to talk things over? Make a decision? Negotiate?"

"There's no need for that," he said without meeting her eyes.

"You didn't," she spat.

"I already bought it," Trent said, although he didn't need to. Emma could read it on his face. Trent had never been good at lying.

"What?!" Emma asked, outraged. "What do you mean you already bought it? We can't live here! I cannot live here, Trent."

Tommy looked up at his parents, concerned.

"Tommy, why don't you go explore the backyard while me and mommy talk."

"Don't send him outside!" Emma shouted, baffled that Trent would say such a thing. "We don't know who or what is out there! Are you crazy?"

"There's nobody out there, Emma! Did you see this place when we pulled in? There's nobody around for miles! That's why we're moving here in the first place. It's safe and quiet."

Emma could not speak. Trent looked down at his son and ruffled his hair. "Go on, bub. Be careful and don't go too far, okay?"

"Awesome!" Tommy shouted, "please let us live here, momma, this is awesome! My room is bigger than our whole apartment in New York! This is way cooler!"

Without waiting for her to respond, Tommy ran through the house and out the back door.

"Why did you do this to me, Trent?" Emma asked through tears. "This is too much."

"How can you think so? Have you seen this place?" Trent raised his arms to take it all in as if it would do anything to change her mind.

"Have *you* seen this place?" Emma countered. "It's falling apart! The floor is gross and peeling, the paint outside is practically nonexistent and we're in the middle of nowhere! Is there even a place to buy food around here? Are we going to have to shop at Walmart?"

"Actually, there isn't even a Walmart for thirty miles, but there is a Shop-N-Save in Coolidge," he said this with a grin on his face, apparently hoping it would make her feel lighter. It wasn't working.

"Look, Emma, I'm sorry I did this without talking to you first, but you always find a way of talking me out of things and I couldn't let you do that this time."

Emma crossed her arms and looked away, too upset to even look her husband in the eyes. Trent tried to put a hand on her, but she shook it off.

"Listen, you know how I am when I write. I need space." He was right. Emma had been with him while he wrote his second novel, *All the Right Reasons*. It had been a tortuous eight months. Every moment he was writing, he was locked in his small office, clicking away. He spent all of his free time researching the topics he used in his story. A character in *All the Right Reasons* was a surgeon, and Trent went so far as to take a six-week course at Columbia University to better understand what goes on in the operating room just so he was satisfied with a chapter in the book. It was overkill, but the book had paid well, and they'd been given a generous advance for Trent to write a third novel.

"The city is too distracting for me. I can't take the noise and the lights and the damn claustrophobia. I just can't anymore. You'll be glad to know I didn't end our lease on the apartment. We can still go back and stay in it, but at least until I finish this book, we're going to stay here. So, be on board, please?"

"You bought this house just so we could stay in it for a few months? I know it's your money, Trent, but you must have spent a fortune on a house just to stay long enough to write a book!"

"The housing prices aren't what they are in New York, sweet pea. I got this house and the five acres it sits on for less than what we pay for a year's rent in New York."

"But why? Why here? In the middle of nowhere, Georgia? There's nothing around. You could have at least gotten us something nice."

"We aren't far from Florida and we're close enough to Atlanta if we decide to fly back to New York for a weekend."

"It's old." Emma said, struggling to find new complaints.

"It's vintage." Trent retorted.

"It's dirty."

"It's rustic."

Emma turned away, finally accepting that she was fighting a losing battle. She considered taking the car and driving herself back to the city without Trent, but they had been on the road since early morning and her back was killing her and she was too tired. Besides, she would either have to leave Tommy here with his father, who would be far too busy writing to take care of him or take Tommy with her, meaning she would have to listen to him whine about leaving.

Maybe I can make this work, she thought. *For a few months. Maybe I can talk Trent into letting me return to the city on the weekends to see my friends before he gets too involved in his writing.*

"What about our things?" she asked, a last-minute effort to thwart his plan. She should have known he had already thought of that.

"I've got a moving team on it right now. They're just bringing the essentials for now, of course. My computer desk, my computer and our clothes. They should be here no later than tomorrow afternoon. We brought enough clothes and supplies until then."

"You expect me to use this furniture? It's *used* for God's sake."

"It'll be fine, Emma. We'll get a new mattress if it means that much to you. We can go into town later and do all of that. In the meantime, try to get used to it. I need this, Tommy needs this and frankly, you need this. You've barely left the city in your life. You could use a little southern hospitality. And I'm not talking about that trashy Bravo reality show you watch."

She ignored his insult toward her comfort show. "Oh, like you had growing up in Denver?" she asked sarcastically. "What do you know about southern hospitality?"

"I know Denver isn't exactly the middle of nowhere, but it's closer to this than to New York."

Trent put an arm around Emma, and she surprised him by not twisting away. "I think you'll come to enjoy it here. We'll get it looking nice! In the meantime, look out the window and tell me how beautiful it is out there. There are more trees in our yard than there are in all of New York City."

Emma humored him and swiped the curtain aside.

She screamed, shocking Trent into a panic, assuming his son was hurt or an equivalent emergency.

"What? What's wrong?" Trent asked.

Emma pointed down to the windowsill, where a dozen or so flies lay dead. "There's fucking BUGS," she shouted.

"There's bugs in the city too, Emma," Trent said, calm now.

"Not in our HOUSE!"

"That's because our windows didn't open in the apartment. That's just the price you pay for fresh air out here. It's worth it. Now let's go get Tommy and take him into town for some groceries.

****

They spent the rest of the day in a town around ten minutes away. Emma wondered if it could even be called a town. She wasn't sure exactly what made a town different from a village, but she would have referred to Coolidge as a village. According to the sign, the population was only six thousand people. There was a small generic grocery store where they bought a few days' worth of food and toiletries, then new linens for the beds. The linens were cheap for her taste, but the small furniture store where they planned to buy a mattress was closed and she would be damned if she was going to sleep on the bed in their room as it was.

They went to a pizza and pasta place in town where the boys gouged on pizza and breadsticks while Emma picked at a salad. Trent, a heavy-set man, was always eating like garbage and it pained Emma to see him sharing the habit with their son, who she was determined to raise to eat as healthy as she did. She let it slide today because even she was finding it hard to listen to her own complaining.

The time was now after 11:00 pm and Trent lay next to her, snoring. She had not so much as drifted off. She was more awake now than she usually was throughout the day. She supposed it was because she'd slept for the last two hours of the drive earlier that day, but there was more to it. Having spent her life in the city, she'd grown accustomed to the noise of passing cars, honking, and the stir of other residents in her apartment building as a kind of ambiance. It helped her to sleep, knowing there were always other people nearby. Out here in nowheresville, the only noise she heard was the stir of crickets outside. She could hear each gust of wind and the effect it had on the old wooden house. It seemed to move with the wind, creaking and cracking. She was attuned to every small sound it made, often feeling panicked, feeling as if someone were certainly in the house, wandering around and causing the noises. She'd woken up Trent twice, who did his best to assure her there was nobody in the house and saying, rather condescending if you asked her, that "old houses just make noises like that". She'd given up seeking his reassurance, but it did little to help her sleep.

Feeling thirsty, she swung her feet off of the bed and walked downstairs to the kitchen. She made sure the front door was locked on her way past. It was.

She pulled a bottle of water from the refrigerator, refusing to drink from the tap. She used the opportunity to take in the house by herself. She tried to look at it from a different perspective. She supposed a large percentage of people in America lived in homes like this. Of course, they lived there because they had to, but still, if they could do it, she could do it. She had never been one to turn down a challenge. Hell, being married to Trent was a challenge of its own. He was overweight and nerdy, unlike any of the men she'd dated in college. She was the opposite of him, athletically built and took great care of how she looked. She was academically smart and excelled in college, but more out of necessity than because she enjoyed it. She'd never been a reader, let alone interested in marrying an author. She sometimes felt bad when Trent got excited with a new idea for a book and talked to her about it. Personally, she didn't care for his writing. She didn't have the heart to tell him she wasn't even a fan of his when they'd met. She'd gone to his book signing six years ago because her friend had invited her. To this day, she has still never read *Better Left to Fray*. She did read a few of his short stories from the *US and the Night* anthology in preparation for their first date, but never anything since.

    He loved her and provided for her, and it was all she could do to pretend the feelings were mutual. She supposed she *had* been charmed by his intelligence and dedication in the first couple of years, but when he wrote his second novel *All the Right Reasons,* she understood just how dedicated he was. She had to do practically everything around the apartment and with their son, who Trent was grooming to be every bit as nerdy as his father. Trent had named him after T.S.

Elliot, for Christ's sake. Thomas Elliot Sinster. She wasn't enthused about the name, but Trent would not relent and promised she could name their next one. She agreed to the terms, withholding the fact that she had no plans of conceiving again. Unbeknownst to Trent, Tommy had been an accident, an example of how birth control is only so effective. To avoid another mishap Emma slept with Trent as little as possible. The sex was laughable, especially compared to the athletic boyfriends she had while in school. But the money he made was enough to allow her to do pretty much anything she felt like. She just had to put up with *him and* pretend to be the model wife and mother. It was a lot to ask of someone who never planned on being either unless the price was right. And until now it had been. Being married to an overweight, work-obsessed nerd was bearable when she had the city and its endless distractions, but was being dragged out into hillbilly country worth it? She supposed she could give it a shot. She would either get used to it and be more comfortable or eventually break down and leave. The fact that the apartment was still there, waiting for them in New York was enough to make her feel a little better. Like a safety net. She could try to cope with her new surroundings the best she could but the first time she woke up with ladybugs in her hair or their house got broken into by meth addicts on ATVs, she was out, with or without the boys. She could always divorce her husband and get a decent check out of it. Of course, he'd be worth more after a few more books-

A creak sounded from above her, pulling her from her revere. She looked up and felt her heart race, only to calm herself down by remembering Trent's words earlier. *There is nobody around for miles.* She hoped he was right. Besides, she'd just checked the door and had checked the windows before going to bed. What made her so worried? She wasn't sure, but something just didn't feel right. She chugged the water bottle, threw it in the trash, then went back upstairs and snuggled against Trent for the first time in a long time.

****

The next morning, Emma awoke alone. She'd somehow managed to snooze through a few hours of dreamless sleep. The sun was coming through the window above her, which had been opened while she slept. It was warm in the house already, but a cool breeze drifted into the window and sent the curtain flapping gently against the sill. It was the first time she had felt at peace since being in the house, until she wondered where Trent was.

She got out of bed and checked her phone that was plugged into the wall and rested on the bedside table. It was after nine! As a rule, she never sleeps past six am. She liked to get up and go down into the gym in her building for a run. Because they'd left so early in the day yesterday, she didn't have a chance to and was now dying to get some exercise. She undressed from her nightgown and put on her leggings and a sports bra.

Peering out of the window, Emma could see Trent and Tommy outside in the backyard. Tommy was sitting on a tire that was suspended from a tree by rope above the ground by about three feet. Trent was pushing him, and Tommy was shouting with joy. Emma almost shouted at Trent to get their son off of that filthy thing but chose not to. If their son got filthy out there in the dirt, Trent could clean him up.

She went downstairs and caught a whiff of bacon and eggs, evidence of them having breakfast without her. She went out the back door and confronted father and son.

"Look mommy, a tire swing!" Tommy said, then shouted with glee as Trent pushed him higher.

"Want a turn?" Trent said with a teasing smile that she found maybe a little handsome.

"No, thanks," Emma replied. "Thanks for letting me sleep all morning." She meant it sarcastically, but it went unnoticed to Trent, who pushed Tommy even higher on the swing.

"No problem. I knew you didn't sleep well last night so I figured I wouldn't wake you."

"How did you know I didn't sleep well?" she asked, crossing her arms.

Trent shrugged. "Because you didn't wake up this morning, I guess." She uncrossed her arms. *Fair enough.*

"Tommy was up when I got up, so we made some breakfast and came outside. I left you a plate in the microwave."

"Thanks, but I think I'm going to go for a run before I eat anything. Do you think there's a gym in that town we went to last night?"

"Who needs a gym?" Trent asked, scoffing, "Just run down the road."

"And end up in *Wrong Turn 3*? I don't think so."

"Well," Trent said, pushing Tommy again and then scratching his chin, "I think we drove by a park in town that looked like it had plenty of shade. There's probably a running track there."

"That'll do. Where are the keys?"

****

Emma drove into town and circled around the streets endlessly searching for the park before finally parking in the lot of the grocery store they'd shopped at the day before and getting out. It didn't really matter where she ran. She could run around the town if she had to, at least there would be other people around and she could get a good look around the town she would need to become familiar with if she were to live in it for any length of time. She took a swig of water, tightened her ponytail, started her music, then took off. She instantly felt better, as if all of the stress and anger she'd built over the last two days traveled from her mind to her feet and out onto the pavement. She turned down one street onto another, careful to remember her way so as not to forget her way back to the car. Everyone who saw her seemed to stare, but not in an impolite way. Most nodded or waved and Emma ignored the first few, but remembered she had an image to keep, even to the hillbillies, and brought herself to wave and even mutter greetings to the people she passed on the sidewalk.

****

When she arrived back home, another car was in their driveway. She could see Trent on the porch next to an older woman, and the two seemed to be in deep conversation. She parked and walked up to greet them.

"Speak of the devil," she heard Trent say, "This is her right here. Emma! You came home just in time. This is Mary. She's a neighbor from down the road. She brought us a gift." He extended a box toward her.

"Oh, I probably shouldn't handle it. I'm smelly and covered in sweat."

The old woman, Mary, waved her arm. "Oh, dear, it won't hurt anything. Go ahead, open it. Tell me how you like it!"

Emma smiled politely and took the box from her husband. She opened it hesitantly, not having the slightest clue as to what it could be.

And she still didn't know what it was after she opened it. It was a mess of cylindrical pipes and strings and a flat piece of wood that held them all together.

"Let me see," Trent said, reaching in and carefully pulling the mysterious item out of its package. He held it by a small hook on top of the wooden plate so that the metal cylinders hung from strings. Pink and blue flowers had been hand-painted onto the metal cylinders.

"It's very pretty," Emma started, "but... what is it?"

"It's a wind chime," Trent answered. He turned to Mary. "Forgive my wife," he said apologetically, "she's lived her whole life in New York City. She's never had a porch before, let alone a wind chime."

"Oh, well that's just fine! See, Emma, wind chimes or wind catchers as some call them, are crafty little things you see a lot out here in the country. They're good luck! And they just sound so pretty. Watch." Mary reached over and pushed gently onto one of the cylinders. It knocked into the one next to it and a high-pitched *ding* resonated from both of them. "On windy days, you'll hear that beautiful sound all day long. They're nature's instruments. I think they're lovely."

"As do we," Trent assured, "thank you so much, Mary. We love it."

****

It was the chime that kept Emma awake that night. Trent had seen to hanging it before Mary left, promising to invite her over for dinner soon. Who was this man? The man next to her pretending to have a wife and son who lived in the country of rural Georgia, making friends with the neighbors and hanging arts and crafts from the porch ceiling and pushing their son on a tire swing as if he wasn't living in a New York City high rise two days ago. It was bizarre to her, and although nothing particularly bad had happened yet, she still wasn't sure if she was on board.

Ding-cling-ding

That damned wind chime. She could hear it all the way up in their second-floor bedroom. How could anyone sleep with that noise? It was loud and obnoxious, possessing none of the soothing, musical qualities that Mary seemed to think it had. She tried to sleep, but every time she dozed off, a breeze would flitter through and set it off. She considered waking her husband and making him go take it down, but knew he would complain and try to justify leaving it up.

Deciding to do it herself, she kicked off her covers and went downstairs and into the kitchen. She grabbed a chair from around the dining room table and dragged it onto the porch. She stood on it in order to reach the hook and plucked the wind chime off of it. The cylinders bounced off of one another and exploded with noise. She hurriedly grasped the cylinders to her chest to silence them and not wake her son. The sudden movement threatened to compromise her balance, and she had to take a quick step off of the chair to avoid falling. She landed hard on her left foot, feeling a terrible sharp pain shoot into her flesh.

"Fuck!" she whisper-screamed. She threw the wind chime onto the ground and watched by way of the moonlight as it landed with a muffled *dink*.

She hopped inside on one foot and sat down on the ancient armchair, sending up a plume of dust. Not caring, she turned on the lamp that was beside the chair and investigated her pain. The cause was a wooden splinter. She felt silly for not thinking to put on her shoes when she got up, but until moving here she never had to worry about getting goddamned splinters if she didn't.

She used her fingernails to pull the splinter from her foot and threw it away. It was when she turned back toward the stairs that she stopped cold. There was someone on the stairs. She'd turned off the light, so it was too dark to see very well. She couldn't tell if it was Trent or Tommy because the figure seemed to be too tall to be her son and too thin to be her husband. Emma couldn't move or breathe.

There was actually an intruder in her house and here she was, downstairs while her husband and son were upstairs. It had them separated. She tried to scream but couldn't seem to find her breath.

Calm down, she said to herself, *I don't even know what I'm looking at. Am I even sure this is a person? It's just something on the staircase. It could be a shadow of something. It must be the thing isn't even moving. But it sure looks like someone is standing on the stairs.*

As if on cue, the figure shook its head as if disappointed in her, then turned to face the second story before taking silent steps up the stairs. Suddenly, her maternal instincts kicked in and all thoughts went from herself to her son alone in his room.

"Hey!" she screamed, racing up the stairs toward the person. She was up the stairs in no time but found herself there alone. She went straight to Tommy's door and flung it open. He was there, sleeping peacefully in his bed.

The bedroom, she thought, then turned toward her room. But she didn't need to go that far to find the intruder. The dark figure had been standing behind her, inches from her face, when she turned around. Emma tried to run backwards but caught her ankle on the doorframe of Tommy's room and fell back, smashing her head against the hardwood floor. Her vision doubled and began to darken. The last thing she saw before the darkness closed in was the face of a woman not much older than herself, looking at her and shaking her head judgmentally.

****

Emma woke up in bed at six o'clock sharp when her alarm went off. She bolted upright in her bed and instinctively reached for Trent. He was there, still asleep.

"Trent," she screamed, "Trent! Wake up!"
Trent scrambled out of sleep and looked at her questioningly.

"Someone was here last night. A lady."
Trent looked at her like she was crazy. "What?"

"Someone was here! I saw someone last night, in the house! Go check on Tommy, quick!"

Trent did not look convinced but lazily rolled himself out of bed and took himself across the hall. Emma could see Tommy's door through the crack of hers and watched as Trent looked in and turned back to her with a thumbs up. She felt relief roll over her.

Trent returned to the room. "What is all of this about?" he asked. He had his hands in his pajama pants and was apparently still half asleep as he kept his eyes half open.

"I got up in the middle of the night," Emma began, "and I went downstairs and I, uh..." the details of the night were growing blurry in her mind the way dreams fade within the first few minutes of waking up.

"I got a chair, and I was standing on it, but I don't remember why. But I got a splinter in my foot. And then I saw a woman on the stairs, but I didn't know it was a woman until I chased her upstairs and she scared me, and I fell over."

"What did she look like, this woman?" Trent asked. She couldn't tell if he was genuinely interested or not and wondered why it mattered.

"I don't really know, I only got a good look for a second. She was our age, maybe a little older. Thirties. That's about all I can say."

Trent pursed his lips, obviously amused and not wanting to laugh. Emma didn't blame him. The story sounded more ridiculous the longer it went on.

"Right, and at what point did you climb back into bed?"

Emma hadn't thought about that. Surely, she wouldn't have experienced something as terrifying as that and then simply climbed back into bed.

"Honey, I think you had a nightmare," Trent suggested. He was trying not to sound condescending. She wanted to deny it but was already starting to consider it.

"But my head hurts. From when I fell over."

"Or because you haven't been sleeping very well."

He had a point, she supposed, but she wasn't quite convinced. She brought her foot from beneath the covers and studied it. There was nothing there to suggest an injury, although splinters usually only penetrated the outer layer of skin and healed quickly. She inhaled a deep breath and rubbed her hands across her eyes.

"It felt so real, though. But maybe you're right." She was starting to feel better already, until a breeze came through and made the curtains shift in the wind. From outside, she heard the *cling-ding-ding* she'd come to despise.

"The wind chime! That's why I was standing on the chair. I was taking down that stupid fucking wind chime. It was keeping me up all night!"

"I guess that settles it, then," Trent replied without much alarm.

"What do you mean?"

"Well, if the wind chime is still there, it's probably safe to say you weren't up in the night taking it down or chasing ghost women around the house."

"I never said it was a ghost." Emma said hatefully. "I thought it was an intruder."

"Well, *I* don't think it was anything. Are you going to get out of bed or what?"

Emma couldn't believe Trent was behaving this way. He was usually timid and quiet, even with her. He usually agreed with whatever she said, as if he still felt the need to impress her. As if her interest in him would expire if he didn't keep her happy at all times. Little did he know that what little interest she ever had for him was long gone and she'd stayed only to maintain her care-free lifestyle in the city, which she didn't even have anymore. She wouldn't sit there and be gaslighted by Trent but also couldn't think of a good way to continue her side of the argument. Maybe he was right this time. It could have been a nightmare, she supposed. The wind chime was still up, her foot was fine, and her headache could be a result of the lack of sleep. She could remember sitting up all night and dozing off in between gusts of wind that sent the chimes into a fury of sound, but it was possible that the noise had worked its way into her dream and her unconscious imagination had taken it from there.

"Now that we have my desk and computer in the spare room, I think I'm going to start brainstorming today. My publisher wants me to do something a little different this time."

"Different how?" Emma asked, although she rarely probed Trent about his writing.

"He says my thrillers are great, but this time, he wants me to write something *psychological*."

"What are you going to call it?" Emma asked. Trent was the kind of author who was great at picking names, and usually had one picked before he even started writing.

But this time must have been different, because he answered with: "I don't know yet."

****

Emma went to town to run again and returned by 9:00 am. She didn't see Tommy in the yard when she arrived. She walked into the house that seemed as empty as three days ago when they'd moved in. She wandered around downstairs before going upstairs, glancing into Tommy's bedroom before pressing her ear to the door of Trent's office. She heard him clicking away at his computer a million miles a minute. She hated to interrupt him while he was deep in thought but worry about not knowing her son's whereabouts was mounting. She still couldn't believe Trent was okay with just letting him roam around outside unattended. She knocked on the door gently. She heard the pounding onto the keyboard stop. A second later, the door opened, and her husband stepped out, shutting the door behind him. He was smiling from ear to ear.

"Hey there, how was your run?"

"Fine. Where's Tommy?" she asked.

"Outside," he answered. "Look through the bedroom window, you should be able to see him."

She stepped into their bedroom and peered out the window, spotting her son on the far end of the yard against a tree line, seemingly exploring. The longer she looked, the more she was convinced there was someone with him. She could just make out another shape walking with him, a little taller.

"See him?" Trent asked.

"I do," Emma responded, "but it looks like someone is with him. Who is it?"

"Oh, her name is Cindy. Remember Mary from down the road? When she was here yesterday, she mentioned bringing her niece over to play with Tommy. She's a little older, but she's sweet. She's very nice to him." Emma wasn't sure how she felt about some random neighbor kid playing with her four-year-old son but was too sick of complaining to Trent that she decided to trust him on this one. Despite what she thought of him, she couldn't deny he was a good father, at least when he wasn't too involved in his writing to pay attention.

Emma jumped when she felt Trent's hand touch her bottom, which was still poking out as she was bent over to look out the window. Trent wasn't often touchy with her; he was usually too timid to initiate sex. She was surprised when he pulled her to him, kissing the side of her neck and gripping her breast.

It had been a long time; she couldn't help but moan.

"Trent, I'm sweaty. Let me take a shower."

"Don't worry about it," he said, pressing himself into her. This was unlike him in every way. She was surprised enough when he came out of his office smiling. He was usually irritated when she bothered him and even when he came out on his own most days, he was too tired or caught up in his thoughts to do anything but go to bed. He was different now, happy that she was home and unafraid to put his hands on her. It was like she was standing in her room with a totally different man. Which is what set her off. She bent across the bed and slid down her leggings, allowing Trent to do as he pleased.

****

The sex wasn't the best she ever had, but the best she'd ever had with Trent. She'd actually orgasmed, which was more than she could say about the last five years of sleeping with him. He usually beat around the bush, hinting that he was horny and leaving it up to her to decide if she wanted to entertain him. Today, he had taken charge for once and it had been magnificent.

They now lay next to each other in bed and snuggled, something they had never done during the light of day. She didn't mind being next to him now as they both lay sweaty and stinky on the sheets. Feeling inspired to share how she felt, Emma opened up.

"I don't think I can live here much longer, Trent," she said.

Trent rolled to his side to face her. "Why not?" he asked.

"I'm not sleeping well. I worry too much about Tommy. I miss the city. The people in town just stare at me. It's too weird here."

"You just have to get used to it, honey. It's a huge adjustment and I'm sorry I threw it at you so abruptly, but I think it will be good for you. Look how good it's been for Tommy. He loves it here. He never got to just run around and play outside in New York. You're just… under-stimulated."

"Maybe. I'm used to being in a busy environment. There's nothing for me to do out here besides keep house and we both know I'm not great at that stuff."

"You're a great mom and a great wife," Trent rebutted. She felt a tear stinging in her eye because she knew it wasn't true. She was a terrible wife who fantasized about leaving her husband and having affairs with handsomer men. Even though Trent was the one who worked, he also did the majority of the parenting when he wasn't writing. "We just have to find something for you to do. Maybe you could open a store in town."

"How am I supposed to do that?" she asked.

"Hello?" Trent taunted, "you have a business degree from Columbia. That should be enough to open a shop in small town Georgia. You can do it, Emma, you just have to forget about being a spoiled city girl."

She scowled at him, but knew he was right. It would be hard transitioning from a city girl in a high-rise apartment in New York City to running a store in the middle of nowhere.

They heard the downstairs door close and feet running up the stairs. Trent and Emma scrambled to conceal their nudity under the blanket just in time for Tommy to appear in their doorway. His hair was crazy as if someone had ruffled it and his clothes were dirty. For the first time, Emma found it cute instead of appalling.

"Cindy left," Tommy said. "Is it time for lunch?"

****

The rest of the day went by in a blur. Emma was the happiest she'd been since arriving. She was glad Trent didn't lock himself back into his office like he usually did once he had a project started. The three of them actually played outside after dinner like a real family, Emma even taking a brief turn on the tire swing after insistence from her son and husband, screaming and laughing as she left the ground behind and soared toward the sky, then came back down. It was only when it came time for bed that her good mood dissipated. She tried to stall going to bed by offering Trent another round of sex, which he gladly accepted, but once they were done, he had fallen to sleep instantly and left her with her thoughts, the sound of the wind, and the *clink-dink-dink* of the wind chime on the porch. She considered placing her headphones in but had never had luck falling asleep to music and needed them to be charged when she ran in the morning. She snuggled against Trent and was about to drift off when she heard footsteps from outside their door.

Her heart sank. Her mouth went dry.

"Trent," she whispered, poking her husband. He groaned, but did not wake up. *There's nobody out there,* she said to herself. *I'm awake this time. Go out there and see for yourself.*

She slid from bed quietly and stepped toward the door, opening it slowly. She peeked out as it opened and saw the same figure from the night before. It was a woman only a little older than herself. The moonlight spilling from the bedroom window made its way to her face, making Emma gasp and pull a hand to her chest. The woman lifted a finger and pointed it at her and said in a voice that was shaky and unused for a long time, "Son…"

Tommy!

Emma snapped out of it and screamed for her husband. "Trent!" she raked her arm across the wall and found the light switch, throwing it on. Light instantly flooded the hallway, but the woman was gone.

Trent was at her side in a second, holding Emma as she sank to the floor. "What is it?" he asked her. She grabbed his nightshirt.

"Sh-sh-she was back" Emma stammered, "the woman from last night. She was in the hallway between our bedrooms just like yesterday. She said something! She said 'son'. Tommy, go check on Tommy!"

"Honey, calm down," Trent said smoothly, "look in front of you."

Emma whipped her head forward and saw Tommy, perfectly fine, standing in his doorway wrapped in his favorite blanket.

"Did mommy have another nightmare?" her son asked.

"I think so, buddy. Go back to bed."

"What?" Emma asked, astonished. "It was *not* a nightmare. I was perfectly awake. We can't stay here; we're leaving right now!"

"No!" Tommy shouted.

"Leaving? We can't leave," Trent said. "You just had another nightmare or maybe sleep paralysis."

"Excuse me?" Emma said. "I was standing in the hallway! I couldn't have been asleep! I have entertained this for too long, Trent, either we're leaving or I'm leaving."

"Nobody is leaving," Trent stated in an unfamiliarly firm tone. "Emma, you're stressed from the move and-"

"Oh, no you don't," Emma interrupted, "You may have gaslit me into staying yesterday but not this time."

"Why are you so intent on ruining this for us?" Trent asked, sounding angry for the first time in their relationship.

"Because" she shouted, matching his energy, "we are not alone here, Trent!"

Trent looked away from her. An expression lit his face. It was a look of excitement, like someone who had just come across the answer to a riddle he had been studying for a long time.

"What's your problem?" Emma asked. "Why are you making that face?"

"It's nothing," Trent said, clearing his throat. "Just come back to bed for tonight and we'll look at this in the morning after we've had some rest. Get up."

She wasn't sure why, but she didn't argue with him. It may have been his tone; it suggested there was no room for argument. Emma had always felt like she was the boss of their relationship but now felt like she was losing control of her husband. She couldn't imagine why he wanted to stay here after all she had been through. Was uprooting their comfortable lifestyle back home and moving them here really so important to him? Well, it wasn't to her. In the morning, she was leaving whether he came with her or not.

****

Emma got out of bed the next morning and dressed to go running. She had not slept at all after returning to bed. Her mind would not leave behind what she'd seen throughout the night. What did the woman in the hall want with her son? *"Son…"* The haunting voice replayed itself all the way until the light of the rising sun signaled, she was clear to get up without suspicion.

She ensured Trent was sleeping soundly and quickly dressed in casual clothes instead of her usual running attire.

I'm getting answers today, she told herself. She left the room and gently closed the door behind her. She considered taking Tommy with her, thinking it would put her at ease, but decided not to. It would take too long, and Trent was sure to wake up soon. He always did. Besides, she feared her new version of a husband would not let her leave with Tommy, even just to go to town. It would be better to pretend to be out on her morning run than to let him know what she was really up to. Besides, Tommy and Trent would be here when she got back. They were both too attached to this place to leave it.

Emma drove to town, straight to Rhonda the realtor's office. It was still early in the morning, and she expected to have to waste some time, perhaps getting a coffee she desperately needed, but she didn't have to wait a single minute. Rhonda had apparently gotten to work early, and Emma caught her just as she was walking inside.

"Rhonda!" Emma shouted, hoping to catch the woman before she made it inside. Rhonda jumped, nearly dropping her mug and a stack of folders she carried.

"Oh my, you scared the devil out of me," Rhonda said. When she recognized who scared her, she said, "Emma! What are you doing here so early? Is everything okay?"

"Not really," Emma said truthfully, "I was hoping to talk to you really quick. Do you have a few minutes?" Rhonda agreed, and invited Emma in to sit down.

"What's going on?" Rhonda probed.

"I never thought I would say this," Emma said. She prepared herself for what was coming next. "I think our house is haunted."

Rhonda, who had looked anxious until this point, let out a long sigh of relief. "Emma," she said, "I never took you to be the superstitious type."

"I'm not," Emma said, embarrassed, "Trust me, I think I've ruled out all other options. I just want some confirmation. Can you tell me if someone ever died on the property?"

Rhonda stiffened in her chair. She seemed like she didn't want to answer Emma. "As a matter of fact, someone did. But Emma, it was over twenty years ago."

Emma couldn't speak for a moment. Although she had expected this news, part of her had hoped Rhonda would answer contrary to her suspicions and put her at ease. Hearing this confirmation was devastating.

"Was it a woman?" Emma asked.

Rhonda was hesitant but nodded her head in agreement.

"About my age, maybe a little older?"

Rhonda didn't even shake her head this time, but her silence was enough.

"Why didn't you tell us?" Emma demanded.

"Because, frankly, I didn't have to." Rhonda replied with a hint of snark. "The state of Georgia does not require a seller to disclose a death in the home unless specifically asked."

"Which is why you are so reluctant to talk to me, right?"

Rhonda shrugged apologetically. "And besides, your husband is well aware of the death that occurred in the home."

"What?" Emma asked. It was not like Trent to keep secrets from her, not anything like this. "What do you mean?"

Rhonda fidgeted uncomfortably. "Look Emma. I feel bad for you; you left the life you loved to come out here with Trent. It isn't right that I should keep some more information from you, but I'm afraid I've told you all that I can for the time being. Trent asked me not to tell you about the death in the house, okay? He said it would deter you from moving here and, well, it only makes sense that I did what I needed to do to sell the house. It's my job. Please don't be upset."

"Upset?" Emma screamed, outraged. "You and my husband have been keeping secrets from me and putting my and my son's life in danger and you don't want me to be upset?"

"Putting your son's life in danger?" Rhonda asked, looking genuinely concerned, "Whatever could you mean by that?"

"The ghost! Or whatever she is! She's been snooping around our room and my son's room and last night she pointed straight at me and said 'son...' like some cryptic fucking *ghoul!*" She was breathing heavily now.

Rhonda stood from her desk and came around to hug Emma, who wanted to shake the woman off but also embrace the comforting gesture even if it came from the source of her anger.

"Listen Emma," Rhonda said, in a calming voice that angered Emma further, "things are not as they seem. Your son is *not* in danger, okay? But this is a conversation you need to have with your husband. Go back home and ask him about it, okay?"

Emma nodded and turned without a goodbye, leaving the office and the town behind as she drove home. Tears of anger filled her eyes, making her drive slowly and impatiently.

When she finally arrived home, she yelled for Trent and Tommy, neither of which answered. "Trent!" She shouted again. There was no response. With a sense of urgency, she raced to the stairs and climbed them, bursting straight into Trent's office as it was the closest room to the top of the stairs and the one she thought Trent was most likely to be in.

The room was empty. The light was off, and the curtains were drawn, but his computer screen was lit, a word document opened. It was in the middle of a page full of words that seemed to blur together. In front of the computer was a notebook she recognized as the one Trent always carried with him while he was in the midst of writing, in case they were out of the house, and he was struck with an idea. Her heart dropped as she read what was written.

```
Anxiety high
Paranoid Ranting
Nightmares
Not Sleeping
"Woman" in the house
"Son"
```

There was more, several pages worth of short bullet points that seemed to summarize her behavior over the last week since moving into the house.

"What the fuck?" she asked herself. "What is this? Is he taking-" suddenly her train of thought derailed. *That's exactly what he's doing. That son of a bitch! He's taking notes!*

It was just like him to be extremely involved in his work, diving into research and spending days or weeks studying to understand the subject he wrote about. But this was too far. He had purposely moved her into a haunted house with the sole purpose of exposing her to the paranormal, then studying how she reacted to it.

Emma grabbed the mouse and used the roller to scroll up to the top of the document. She almost laughed a hysterical, this-is-not-funny-at-all type laugh. It was titled *We Are Not Alone.*

That motherfucker!

Just then, she heard Tommy giggle from his bedroom, bringing her out of her thoughts. She had to get Tommy and get him out of here now! Fuck Trent and his stupid house.

She turned to exit the office, slamming right into her husband's stomach.

"Emma," he said, "Cindy, Tommy and I were playing in his room. We didn't expect you back so early." He looked at her outfit. "Did you change already?"

"I didn't go running." Emma said, then felt silly. She didn't need to explain herself to him right now. He needed to be the one to explain. "What is this, Trent? Is this some kind of experiment for your new book? You're keeping me prisoner here in this house so you can study me? Do I look like a fucking guinea pig to you?"

Trent peered past her into the office, seeing his mistake. "Ahh," was all he said. "I was hoping you wouldn't see that."

He seemed so casual, a fact that Emma wasn't sure how to feel about.

"Well," he said, finally, "You got me."

Emma shook her head in disbelief. She was suddenly infuriated. That's all he was going to say?

"'I got you'? What does that mean?"

"That's what I was doing. I'm sorry, Emma, but my work is very important to me. When my publisher wanted something different from me, the idea for this excited me too much. I knew you'd never let me move here under any circumstances, but especially if you knew about the haunting. I asked Rhonda not to mention it when we met the other day."

"I know," Emma spat, "I've spoken with her already."

"Then you're caught up," Trent stated blankly.

"No, "Emma said. "There's more. I know there is. I can see it. I can tell by your face." She could. His face was guilty and gave her the idea that she had found out some but not all of the information. He had always been a terrible liar, and she knew this look when she saw it.

"I know there's more to this," she said, "this whole thing still doesn't make sense. Why did you pick this house? We lived in New York; how did you find out about this place all the way in Georgia." It was a question she'd thought to herself before even moving in, but decided she didn't care enough to ask. "And if the realtor wasn't going to disclose the fact that someone died here, how did you know someone did?" She was asking the right questions. She watched his face as she spoke, confident that she was on the right track.

"I'm not sure where to start," Trent said, his voice barely loud enough for her to hear. After a heavy silence, he reached past her and turned on the light for the office. When they could see better, Trent placed his index finger against the wooden door frame. Emma followed it and saw what he was pointing at. It was his name, scratched into the wood, with several horizontal dash marks beneath it. Something she'd seen done in movies to track a child's growth.

"Who did that?" she asked, her voice shaking and her heart thumping.

"My mother did," Trent answered, "When I was eight."

Emma didn't understand. "But how is that possible? You... you grew up in Colorado!"

"Not exactly," Trent sighed. "I was born here in Georgia. In this house, actually. I lived here until my mother died. She was murdered by my dad. He was a drunk and a mean one at that. My mom tried to stop him from beating me half to death one night, and he turned his anger on her. She was killed trying to protect me. My dad died in prison, and I went to live with my aunt and uncle in Denver."

"Those are your parents, I've met them, Trent!"

"I call them mom and dad, sure, but they aren't my real parents." Trent said this slowly as if Emma was a child younger than their own. "I always wanted to come back here. So much so that I contacted the owner a few months ago. I told him I was interested in buying the house, but not why. He told me I didn't want it. You know why? Because there's a 'depressing vibe' as he put it. He said he could swear he heard a woman's voice, crying in the night. Footsteps around the house. I knew it had to be my mother, alone and heartbroken after everything that happened when I was so young. I knew I had to come back. He agreed to sell me the house after I made an offer he couldn't refuse. I just asked that he make some updates and renovations so that you would be more comfortable. I know that it isn't perfect to you, but it is to me."

Emma could not believe this. Could it be true? It was absolutely insane, but it did answer her questions. There was just one thing she couldn't get over.

"So that means that *thing* I keep seeing is…" Emma trailed off, not sure if she could say it.

Trent nodded. "Cynthia Sinster, born 1970. My late mother. She was not much older than us when she was murdered. I was the light of her world. And now, Tommy is, too. I know it doesn't seem like she likes you, but that's just how mothers are. She'll come around if you both try. We can have a family here, Emma. All four of us."

Emma stood perfectly still. Suddenly the air around her felt too thick to breathe. Ghosts were supposed to be anonymous. Just bumps in the night, a footstep here and a door closing there.

"Come on. Let me show you," Trent said gently.

Emma wanted nothing less but found her muscles too weak and her curiosity too strong. She forced every breath in and out as she walked across the hall to her son's room, where she could still hear him giggling and laughing.

Emma reached the door first. Trent opened it, then stepped aside so Emma could see what was beyond.

What she saw terrified her. The dark shape she'd seen during the night was in her son's room, hovering several feet off of the ground. Her son threw her a ball and she caught it, then threw it back. Tommy reached his little arms out and the figure grabbed him under the arms, raised him into the air and swung him around, flying across the room with him. He squealed with delight.

Caleb S.

Trent cleared his throat, catching the attention of his mother and son. The specter stopped in mid-air and floated slowly toward the ground. Her eyes met Emma's, and Emma felt a hatred like nothing she'd ever felt before emanating from her.

"Mom," Trent started, "I'd like you to meet my wife, Emma".

But Emma was no longer there. Looking at the ghost had broken her trance and given her the motivation to run. She screamed a blood curdling howl as she descended the stairs. She went straight for the car and threw herself in it. The car was leaving the driveway by the time Trent made his way outside.

"Emma, wait!" He shouted. "I wanted us to be a family! Stay, please!" It was no good. She was long out of earshot.

Trent returned to the house, tears spilling onto his face. Tommy met him on the porch, leaving the ghost of his grandmother to watch from the window of his bedroom. Tommy hugged his father around the legs.

"It's okay, dad. Grandma says mommy wasn't any good for you, anyway."

"I know," Trent said, "but I was hoping things would still work out." With his arm around Tommy's shoulder, father and son went back inside the house, their family still incomplete.

The Diggins

The sun was setting over an empty town. An empty country. An empty world. Empty houses lined the streets of Hermoso Lugar, California, a city once bustling with 100,000 people as of the 2016 census. With the sun's dramatic descent came an array of beautiful colors that had enticed those thousands of residents to call the city their home. But tonight, the view went to waste, as dozens of sunsets had before it.

Okay, so the town wasn't entirely empty. There was one resident left. A boy of ten named Henry. He didn't see the sunset, however, because even though he was no longer afraid of encountering other desperate survivors, he still made it a habit to be inside before sunset.

Henry didn't know why he survived. He didn't like to think about it, but the nightmares he had every night kept the memories of what happened fresh.

He remembered the warnings over the radio and television that a disease was spreading, and a few weeks later his parents stopped going to work. People started to panic, buying all of the toilet paper and frozen food from stores. His father used to complain that the entire thing was made up, until more people started to get sick, and more people began to die. His grandmother was the first to die in his family, and he hardly had time to grieve before his grandfather died shortly after. By this time there was no school, which he didn't mind, but found himself missing it when things got worse. It seemed that anyone who caught the disease died within days, so people were doing all they could to gather food and supplies to isolate themselves in their homes, including stealing their items from local stores or even their neighbors. Henry's father was a Marine veteran, and told his family the National Guard was setting up places for them to go if they needed protection, but the streets were too backed up with families going to the same place that thieves began attacking them and Henry's dad drove away when they heard gunshots. Back at home, Henry's parents argued about what to do. They only had enough food to last a week or two if they really stretched it out. They couldn't get more because by now the stores were surely empty and nobody in their right mind would share with them.

    This was when Henry's mother had an idea. She was a librarian at the Hermoso Lugar Public Library, and told her husband, "The library. We need to go to the library."

    "Yes," his father replied, "What we really need right now is some John Grisham."

    "No!" his mother shouted, "The food drive! The library has been taking donations for months that we were going to give away on Thanksgiving! My god, Richard, there must be months' worth of food in there!"

    It hadn't taken his father any further convincing. They waited until the cover of darkness was upon them and snuck the five blocks to the library as quietly as possible. Henry could remember how eerily quiet the streets were then. He wasn't out much after dark, but he was smart enough to know that not everyone went to bed at 8pm like he did. There were people who worked at night and drove at night and played music and drank beer and went on walks. But not anymore.

    When they reached the library, Henry's mother used her key to let them in. For Henry, being at the library was better than being at home. It was a place of comfort for him. He wasn't exactly popular in Mrs. Tomlin's third-grade class. After school he would take the bus to the library and read until his mother was able to drive him home. It was his favorite place, and it did not scare him to be there in the dark like it did in his own bedroom.

What did scare him, though, was that his mother wasn't the only library employee to remember their stockpile of food. Amy Littler, a teen who had a permit to leave school early and work in the library's children section, had also had the idea to wait out the outbreak in the library's basement pantry with her boyfriend. Henry knew her well, because she played with him and was always giving him sweets while he waited for his mother to finish work. She always talked to him in a false, high voice that he knew she only used because he was a kid, but he didn't care because she sounded like the characters in the kid's shows he watched when he was at home, and he liked it.

When Henry's family tried to get through the door of the pantry, Amy's boyfriend stopped them. His father made a feeble attempt to reason with the couple, suggesting they could share the resources, but it didn't work. Amy's boyfriend, a high school senior and varsity football player, knocked Henry's father to the ground before he'd even finished his proposition. A fight broke out while Henry's mother and Amy screamed, and Henry cried. Fortunately, Henry's father may have been getting older, but he had played some football in his own day. He's also dabbled in boxing and had experienced his fair share of tussles. He was able to overcome the teen but showed mercy when he knew the fight was his.

"I'm sorry," he had said to the young man, "but I have to do what is right for my family. You can stay here and share the food, or you can leave. Either way, my family is staying."

"Fuck you," is all the teen said. His pride had been hurt more than anything, and he grabbed Amy by the wrist to lead her outside. She begged her boyfriend to stay, but he was hearing none of it.

Henry's mother suggested they at least give them some supplies for the road, but his father assured her things had gone too far for that.

"If they come back, we'll tell them the offer is still on the table to share. But we don't need to hand them our food to watch them walk away with it. I don't think they'll be back."

Caleb S.

But his father was wrong. They did come back. Seven days later.

In those days, Henry's parents rationed the food and organized the pantry to make it more comfortable for the three of them, since that had essentially become their shared bedroom, and it was not very big. Because the room was in the basement, they allowed themselves to quietly wander outside of the pantry, but going upstairs was strictly forbidden for Henry. He eventually convinced his mother to go up and pick out a couple of books that he could read to pass the time. The first time she went up, she brought back two children's books that he'd already read, but he read them again anyway.

The family had just begun to let their guard down on the seventh day. Henry's mother had even mentioned taking him with her next time she went upstairs to look for books.

The three of them were sitting on the floor of the basement eating canned food (his parents were having canned potatoes while Henry was having Spaghetti-Os) when they heard glass shatter upstairs. Voices made their way down to the basement, and Henry's parents jumped into action to hide the evidence of their hiding place.

"Where's it at?" a male voice asked from above. A girl's voice answered, so low that Henry could barely hear it. She said, "In the basement." She sounded like she was crying.

****

"Henry, come on!" Henry's father whispered.

"No," his mother argued, "This is the first place they'll look. They'll know we're here, Rich, it's over for us." She began to cry. Henry understood. The evidence that someone was living here was too obvious. They had a matter of seconds to try to hide, and it would be for no good. They were trapped in the basement.

"We have to stay here in the pantry," his mother said through tears, "Henry, go hide!"

He wanted to argue, but he also wanted to believe everything would be alright. He didn't argue, instead ran across the basement and hid behind a dusty broken bookshelf that was barely tall enough to conceal him. It was the only place he could reach before the door to the basement opened from above just as his mother closed the door to the pantry.

"Lead the way," the male voice said. He heard light sobs as a girl descended the steps. Henry could see through the spaces between two shelves and figured he was in the dark enough that they couldn't see him.

When the girl came into view, he knew instantly that it was Amy, but only because she was wearing the same clothes from in a week ago. Her face had become unrecognizable. It was gaunt and covered in bruises. Her hair was crazier than a crow's nest, and there seemed to be places on her head where the hair had been pulled out because it was bald and caked in a layer of dry blood. She was never a big girl, but she now looked more like a skeleton with skin than his old friend from the library.

She was followed closely by three men, all much older. To Henry's eight-year-old mind, he had no concept of their age except that they were older than his parents but younger than his grandparents. They all had beards and tattoos and most importantly, guns. He noticed the guns, all long shotguns like the one his dad had let him shoot once over the summer. As Amy stepped into the light, a man asked, "Alright, girlie. Where's the stash?"

Amy let out a sob but nonetheless pointed to the pantry door. She used both arms to do this, which is when Henry realized her hands were tied together.

"Good," one of the men said, "Now go sit over there." He shoved her to the side. She stumbled and fell, then scrambled away with her feet until she was against the wall and as far away from the men as possible.

Henry couldn't take his eyes off of her. His own parents had undoubtedly lost weight over the last week in their effort to make sure Henry had enough to eat but this was different. Amy looked like she hadn't eaten at all since the last time he saw her.

While the men made a half-circle around the pantry door, Amy averted her eyes from what was about to happen. Henry did the same, and their eyes met. There was something in Amy's eyes when he met hers. Something he would recognize later as relief.

She mouthed something to him that looked like *I didn't tell them about you.*

One of the men reached for the doorknob, but the door burst open before he had the chance to turn it. His father, Richard the Marine who boxed as an amateur and had easily bested the high school football player one week ago, was no match for the three men.

He did manage to knock one down, but before he could even turn to face the other two, a gunshot rang out. The sound felt physical, as if it displaced the very air in the underground room. Henry had forgotten just how loud sounds could get as he had spent the last week merely whispering with his family in an effort to keep their presence a secret.

Henry screamed as his father fell to the ground, but fortunately so did Amy and he went unnoticed. His ears were still ringing when the second shot rang out, followed by a high-pitched squeal and moan from his mother that he could barely hear over the ringing in his ears.

That was all it took. The two people he knew the best, the two who knew *him* the best, gone. The ones who he had spent every waking day of his life with, the ones who read him to sleep and bought him Christmas presents and spent the last week eating vegetables out of a can so that he could have the Spaghetti-Os and ravioli he liked so much. They were gone in a matter of seconds.

Henry tried everything not to cry but couldn't help himself. He saw Amy make a shushing gesture out of the corner of his eye, but the men were whooping and hollering with victory and exchanging high fives loudly enough that his whimpers went unheard.

The men raided the pantry and stuffed all they could into a duffle bag one of them had slung over his shoulder. Henry watched as one man opened a can of peaches and drained them with a single gulp, then belched.

"This was a good find, little lady," the man said to Amy. "I may just let you live after all."

"You said you would let me go if I showed you where the food is," she replied.

"Did I?" the man asked sarcastically. "Dan, you remember me saying something like that?"

The man who was stuffing food into the duffle bag grunted, "Nuh uh."

He looked to the other man. "John?" he asked, "do you?"

John shook his head.

"I don't remember saying I would let you go. You're too good at finding us food." At this, his friends all started to chuckle.

"You asshole!" Amy screamed. "Get this fucking rope off of me right now and let me go!"

The man smacked Amy and she fell onto her back. He mounted her, and shouted, "You don't tell me what to do, bitch!" and punched her. The back of her head bounced hard off of the basement floor. The man called Dan said, "Woah man, careful. You're gonna kill her!"

"And so, what? We don't need to be luggin' her around all over the place kickin' and screamin'. Besides, she's just another mouth to feed. I say we take care of her now and leave her here."

"Will, that's crazy." John said, "We can't murder her. She can help us find more food. We need numbers."

"Who the fuck do you think you're talking to? You wouldn't even be here if it weren't for me." Will said.

"I'm just asking you not to do it, man." Dan said in a whiny voice. "We've killed too many people as it is. It's making me sick."

Amy lay beneath Will, covering her bleeding face in case he hit her again.

"If you're so worried about food, why don't you take a bite out of this?" Will asked, then grabbed Amy's arm by the wrist and pinched her arm between his teeth. Amy screamed in pain.

"Hey, Will, stop!" Dan yelled, "You're fucking crazy!" He raised the gun and pointed it at Will. "I'm tired of this shit, get off of her."

Will started to say something but instead exploded off of the floor with an uppercut that knocked Dan squarely on the jaw. Dan hit the ground hard, dropping the gun as he fell. John pounced onto Will, but Will shook him off and threw him to the ground as well. The gun was within John's reach, and he grabbed it, pointing it toward Will and firing. He fired too early, however, and the bullet only clipped him in the side. He stayed standing and grabbed the barrel of the gun out of John's hand and turned it toward him. Will, unlike John, took his time aiming and did not miss when he pulled the trigger. He watched John die, then turned the gun toward Dan, and shot him, too. Then, assuming he was alone, he threw the gun aside and sat against the wall. He winced as he held his wound, looking around for something to bandage it with. He didn't see Amy get off of the floor until it was too late. Before he could react, she had the shotgun pointed at him. He held his arms up in surrender, but didn't get a word out before she pulled the trigger and ended him.

Henry had been too afraid to watch any of this. He waited until he heard Amy's voice telling him it was okay before he came out. He didn't feel the need to remind her that her pants were still off.

"Thank you," Henry said. She didn't say anything, just threw the shotgun aside and held his hand. Her wrists were bloody and bruised and her hands were a different shade than the rest of her arm. He assumed she'd done all she could to wrestle her way out of the rope while the men were distracted fighting each other. Amy picked up the duffle bag full of food with her free hand. She led Henry away from the bodies of the three men and his parents and led him upstairs.

"We can't go up there," Henry said, panicked. "Someone might see us through the windows!"

"Nobody will see us," she said with eerie calm. "There is nobody else out there, Henry. They're all gone. I've been being dragged around by those guys for days. I haven't seen anyone for a long time. They either succumbed to the disease or they left and went somewhere else. I don't know where. That's what Michael and I were trying to do after we left here that night. Trying to get out of the city when those three men downstairs stopped us. They killed Michael right in front of me." She struggled not to cry again. "There is no one else."

They made it upstairs and went to the children's section of the library, where they sat in silence and ate canned Spaghetti-Os. Henry only had one, but Amy had three, plus a can of peaches. She spent a long time in the bathroom and at least five minutes at the water fountain that was, surprisingly, still working.

****

They didn't say much to each other that night. Henry cried a little about his parents, but wanted to keep it together for Amy, who was the one who had actually been beaten up. It didn't seem fair that he should be crying while she sat there next to him, not showing any emotion at all. He wanted his parents back, but if they were gone and the rest of the world was gone, he would rather be with Amy than be alone. He fell asleep in her arms.

****

The next morning, Amy was gone. Henry woke up and didn't feel her next to him. He jumped up and ran into the lobby, then searched the library, still being cautious to not be seen through the windows. He did not go into the basement, but he opened the door and called her name until he was certain she was not down there. When he went back into the children's section of the library, he noticed a piece of paper lying on the ground where she had slept that he must not have seen earlier.

Henry,

I'm leaving tonight. I have to find help. I had to leave in the middle of the night because I knew you would want to go with me and not be left by yourself. But it is better this way. If you came with me and something happened, like what happened to me, I would not be able to forgive myself. I'm hoping that the disease can't survive in the cold of Canada or the heat of Mexico. Maybe I'll find a friendly group of survivors. If I do, I promise to bring them back here as soon as I can to rescue you. Thank you for sharing your Spaghetti-Os with me last night. I hope you don't mind that I took a few cans of food with me before I left. There is still plenty for you to have for a long time. I

also brought up all of the rest of the food from downstairs, so you never have to go back down there.
-Amy

Henry, in his frantic search for Amy, had completely missed the mound of food she had left outside of the entrance to the children's section of the library. He took all of the items and put them in a room that was usually reserved for readings and events for children but was now Henry's new bedroom.

****

That was a while ago. Henry wasn't sure how much time had passed. He found calendars in the library but because he had spent time living in the basement, he wasn't sure what days to cross off or how many had gone by since then. All he knew was it was almost Thanksgiving when everything went wrong, and now the temperature was getting a little bit warmer every day.

He decorated his room with pictures of dinosaurs and racecars and a big map of California he found in the travel section.

Caleb S.

He'd been eager for Amy's return, but she had not come back. Henry spent the first few days still hiding from the view of the windows but had stopped doing that weeks ago. In fact, he had recently taken to going outside. He now knew Amy was right. There was nobody else, not in Hermoso Lugar and not in the world for all he knew.

When his Spaghetti-Os had run out and he was forced to eat the canned fruits and vegetables, he took to the streets to search for more food, preferably something tastier. He never found much, but he always found something.

He always knocked before he went into someone's house. Not because he expected someone to answer, but just because it felt wrong not to. If he saw bodies, he left without looking. The power had been off in the city for many weeks, but in some houses the water or stove still worked, and he was able to warm up his can of green beans and take a bath. He went to his old house sometimes to change his clothes and play with his toys, and even once to take a nap in his old bed, which felt like sleeping on a cloud compared to the library floor. He had since carried his mattress and bedding back to the library on a wagon he used to play with outside.

He always returned to the library before sunset because his parents were there. He couldn't bear the thought of leaving them. His parents, and his books. He'd read at least one book every day. It helped the time pass and kept his mind distracted. He'd started with books from the children's section but soon became bored of them. He decided to find more adult books by authors that his dad liked. He knew his father loved a writer named Stephen King, but the first book Henry looked at was about a disease that killed off most of the world. Henry threw that one in the trash.

Sometimes he read the books out loud, fearing that he might lose the ability to speak if he never had anyone to speak to again. He also spoke to his parents. Not directly, of course. He had considered going downstairs and sitting with his mother and father's corpses to talk to them. He missed them so much that he was willing to look at them in their mutilated and decomposing state if it meant seeing them at all. He had no pictures of them and was afraid he would forget what they looked like. He needed to get a good look at them now before they were too decomposed to be recognizable. The only thing stopping him was the presence of the bad men. Even though they were dead, he was still irrationally afraid of them. Sometimes he wondered if they were still alive after all, waiting for him to walk down the stairs to talk to his parents or search for more food. He didn't want them to grab him and hurt him like they hurt Amy. He often had nightmares of hiding behind the bookcase after they killed his parents and beating Amy's head into the floor.

One morning, he left with his wagon to explore the town again and scavenge for food when he looked to the sky as the sun was still rising. It was a beautiful sunrise, with shades of pink spraying through the morning air. Henry dropped the wagon and walked over to the sign with changeable letters in front of the library doors. It was advertising some book signing event for a day that had undoubtedly already come and gone. He used the letters to spell out "Happy Easter", except it actually said, "Happy   E ster" because there was only one "a".

He wasn't sure if it was Easter or not, but it was probably close enough and the sunrise reminded him of the Easter mornings he had before, when his parents would take him to church and then go back home for a special breakfast.

Deciding he could risk not looking for provisions for one day, he ditched the wagon and went back into the library to celebrate by reading a book and otherwise taking the day off. He felt like mixing things up and went not to his normal area, fiction, but to the non-fiction area on the other side of the library. He searched for several minutes through books about history, war, and cooking and quickly became bored.

There have to be more interesting books around here, he thought. He wandered the library hoping for something to catch his eye.

After strolling down every aisle in the non-fiction section, he stopped before a door that said PRIVATE and underneath EMPLOYEES ONLY. He tried the door, and, to his surprise, it opened. The smell of dank, stale air reached his nostrils, and he breathed it in. The room didn't have a window, but he could see enough to know it was a storage space of some kind. There were shelves of old, dusty books that looked like they hadn't been touched in years. He stepped in and began looking through them, but most were too worn to make out the titles on their spines. On the floor in the center of the room was a box, not in much better condition than the dozen or so books inside of it. On the side of the box were the words "THROW OUT" written in marker. The books in the box were in the worst condition of all. Several didn't have covers, some were stained and unreadable, and one was ripped clean in half.

Henry dug to the bottom of the box and pulled out the book furthest down, held it in the light so he could read the faded title.

The Diggins by Francis Hamilton.

A memory exploded in his brain of his father telling him about what they called *The Diggins*. It was a ghost town in central California, once bustling with the business of gold mining, but long since abandoned. He'd also heard about it in Ms. Bethel's history class this year when they learned about the California gold rush.

He carried the book back to his room in the children's section and sat on his mattress.

Maybe I should take the book down and read it to mom and dad. Dad liked to talk about the diggins. So, what if the bad guys are down there too? They can't hurt me anymore. But he knew that if the bad men couldn't hurt him, his father couldn't listen to him read.

I'll just stay here in my room and read, he decided. He opened the book and read the first page.

In 1850, the gold rush was in full swing. Towns were sprouting up all throughout the deserts of California to house men who came to seek their fortunes. When prospectors flooded the area and began to dig out massive mining operations on the hunt for gold, these areas became known as "the diggins", (get it, kids? Because they were always diggin'!). It's a nickname that persists to this day, at least for the ones who live near enough to carry the tradition. In fact, one prospecting village only 20 miles outside of present-day Hermoso Lugar adopted "The Diggins" as its official name.

The haste in which these villages were established did not leave much room for structure, and most gold mining towns were a lawless wasteland of theft and murder. While some men became rich, others died at the hands of greedy thieves. Without the presence of law enforcement, crime was rampant and not many of these criminals ever saw justice unless it was at the hands of their own neighbors.

By 1855, the gold had been exhausted from most of the area, and the towns were abandoned. They receive thousands of tourists annually, making it a great place to see history with your own eyes.

The Diggins, however, is a particularly interesting town because its gold deposits were generous and continued to provide gold for years after the other mines in the area dried up. Men began to move their families to The Diggins to get comfortable, which made its end all the more tragic.

In 1858, a gang of miners from the failed mines in other areas of California raided the town and broke into the makeshift bank vault to rob them of their hard-earned labor. When the townsfolk fought back, a war erupted, and by the time the sun rose the next morning, nearly half the population of men, women, and children were dead.

You can visit The Diggins today but be warned; you may not want to stay after dark! After all, they don't call it a "Ghost Town" for nothing! Some say the spirits of the old mining town's residents still reside, haunting the land and searching for revenge. Many ghost-hunting teams have reported seeing a shadowy figure guard the entrance to the mine. Some have reported screams coming from houses that were burned during the massacre, and some have even claimed to have seen balls bouncing, as if ghostly children are still out to play before their mamas call them in for dinner.

Every paranormal investigator has at least agreed on one thing – they never feel alone while in The Diggins!

Caleb S.

Henry read the last few words again.
Never feel alone while in The Diggins.
Never feel alone.
Alone.

His heart pounded as he read that word. He knew he was lonely, but not until just now did he realize how lonely. His entire city was a ghost town now. Ghosts used to scare him, but now he thought he would welcome even the presence of the dead if it meant he would have someone to talk to. But if ghosts were real, wouldn't the entire city be full of them? Wouldn't his parents have come back to speak with him? Would the bad men come back and haunt him? He didn't think so. There must be some kind of rules about who became ghosts and who didn't, otherwise everyone would be a ghost after they died. He wasn't sure. What he did know was that he craved interaction more than anything in the world. He wished Amy hadn't left. He would have shared all of his Spaghetti-Os with her until the end of time if it meant he could have a friend. He'd been alone for so long now that he almost cried thinking of it.

If there were spirits, maybe he could talk to them, make friends with them. It would be better than nothing. He was pretty sure he had watched enough scary movies with his dad to know that ghosts could talk, and they weren't always bad, right? He remembered in one of the scary movies, the characters held a seance. When he asked his dead what a seance was, he'd responded, "It's how you talk to people after they're dead."

Talk to people.

He'd almost asked if seances were real but wondered if it might be a stupid question and didn't. *Some* people obviously believe they're real.

An idea struck him hard. One that suggested he go to The Diggins and see for himself. He debated in his mind if he should do it. On the one hand, he had a comfortable shelter here at the library. He had food and a relatively comfortable bed and enough books to last him a lifetime. But he didn't have the sense that he was really doing anything to help himself. Amy had been brave and went to search for help but as much as he hated to think of it, he no longer expected her to come back for him. Plus, despite how much he ignored it, the bodies in the basement reeked. He needed to get out of the library.

I can always come back, he thought, *it isn't really that far away.*

****

He spent the next day searching for something to drive. He thought he knew how, but most of the cars he found were locked, and almost none of the unlocked ones had keys in them, and the ones that did were too big for him and he couldn't see over the steering wheel. He eventually gave up on trying to drive and decided instead to walk. Twenty miles seemed like an eternity to a kid, but Henry knew it would only take two days at most to get there. He packed a week's worth of food and water bottles he'd refilled using the water fountain into the bad man's duffel bag along with his pillow, blanket, and his favorite books. He ripped the map of California off of his wall and threw it with the duffel bag onto his wagon and laughed at the irony of his situation.

With all of his belongings loaded onto his wagon, he set off on foot toward The Diggins, wondering what you're supposed to say to a ghost.

They Need Help

Shawn took one last drag of his cigarette. He didn't smoke regularly, but this occasion nearly called for one. It had been years since his last job interview, and it was all he could do to stop his hands from shaking. He looked at the cigarette and remembered the time he had promised his parents to never do such a thing. Now he wished he had time to start another one. The numbers on the dash of his car read 0754. Time to go inside. Shawn flicked his cigarette and collected his papers, stepped outside, and took a deep breath. He read the massive steel banner atop the building. Although the place seemed surprisingly well kept and the banner said, "Grassy Plains Behavioral Health Center," he could see only dark clouds, a bolt of lightning, and the words "Insane Asylum". He knew these places rarely called themselves that anymore, but deep down they were one in the same.

Shawn made it inside the building and was greeted by a friendly nurse at the reception desk who directed him to the security office. An older man, Shawn guessed to be around sixty, introduced himself as Earl Fitzpatrick: Chief of Security. "How are you today, Shawn?"

Shawn was almost surprised to hear this. For many years he practically had no first name. "I'm fine sir, how are you?"

"Why do you seem so shocked? Forget your name?"

"No sir, I'm just used to being called Myers. That's all."

"Ah, right, you're a military guy," Earl said, unimpressed. He stared blankly at Shawn and looked down at the paper, as if something didn't quite add up.

"How old are you again, Mr. Myers?" he asked.

"Twenty-four, sir."

"Damn, and with a resume like this? How are you twenty-four if you spent five years in the Air Force? Did you join at fifteen or something?"

"Seventeen, sir. There wasn't much of a job market where I'm from and they said they'd pay for my college, so I signed right up."

"Did they? Pay for your college, I mean?"

"Yes sir. All four years. I did it all online while I was stationed in England."

"I see," he said and shuffled his papers. "Well, let's get down to it. I have to say, your resume is quite impressive. Five years Security Specialist in the Air Force, one tour in Iraq, bachelor's in applied science of criminal justice," Earl removed his glasses and put the resume on the table in front of him. "Seems to me like you're a little overqualified to be a security guard at a hospital. What the hell makes you want to work here?"

Shawn thought for a moment before responding. "No offense, Mr. Fitzpatrick, but I've been through a lot over the past couple years and figured I would work a job with a little less stress. Maybe one day I'll go on to become a cop or something, but for now hospital security seems like a bit of a break for me."

"I see," said Earl. He looked away from Shawn and back to his papers.

"You were discharged under less than honorable conditions, Mr. Myers. Now I guess you don't have to elaborate on that, but I have to say I'm curious."

Shawn heard the question Earl didn't ask.

"Well, sir, um…I was seven months into my second tour overseas when my wife, Chloe, was in an accident. She was driving during a severe thunderstorm and ran into a tree across the road." Shawn gulped and struggled to shoo away a tear he felt forming. "She didn't die. Not right away, at least. She was in critical condition though and I tried to get home, I tried so hard. But my request wasn't approved in time and she… succumbed to her injuries. I couldn't get out of Iraq. I missed the funeral. The second I saw my commander I assaulted him. Punched him in the face, for denying my leave. I know it was wrong; I just couldn't help myself. So, when I finished my tour, they gave me the boot."

Earl looked at him with interest. He dropped his gaze and muttered something like "I'm sorry to hear that." Then Earl sat up straight again and said: "Look, we're dying for some good people here. You seem like you'll fit the bill. I'm gonna skip all the normal interview mamba-jamba and say this; I like you!" He threw his hands into the air to exaggerate his point. "I want you here. In fact, I would like to make you an offer you can't refuse. I'm old as dirt, there is no denying that. I've been wanting to retire for fifteen years; I just can't find anyone the hospital admins find worthy to run this pile when I leave. Yeah, I have a few guys working under me already but *you*! You seem like you would fit the bill. This may be more than you bargained for, but I'd like to offer you my job as the Chief of Security. Of course, the hospital administration will have to approve it and all, but I think I can work some magic. Hell, they'll be happy to get me out. What d'ya think?"

"Uh, Mr. Fitzpatrick, I don't know, that seems like a lot. I mean I've never even been here before. How am I supposed to run all of this?"

Earl chuckled. "It's nothing! It's mostly making schedules and other paperwork. I'll show you the ropes, you'll get it in no time." When Shawn didn't answer, he went on. "You still seem unsure, so how about this. I'll talk this all over with the admins and see what they think. If they like it, it's yours. If not, well, we'll hire you as an officer anyway. It's a win-win for you! How 'bout it?"

Shawn thought hard but not long before agreeing to the terms. The two men shook hands and agreed to stay in touch.

****

Shawn got a call less than forty-eight hours later. The admins were apparently just as impressed with Shawn's resume as Earl was, and the job was his, if he accepted it. Shawn did accept the job and returned to the hospital for the paperwork and training. In the meantime, Shawn used Chloe's life insurance to fund the seventy-mile move to Cambria from his home in Millertown. He settled down in a rather large three-bedroom house on an acre of land a short drive from the hospital. It was a house Chloe would have loved.

The death of Chloe had made Shawn what some might consider a rich man, at least in rural Pennsylvania. All of his belongings were transferred with the help of his brothers and a couple of friends and after the last box had been unpacked, the group went out for a celebratory drink. It felt good to Shawn. He hadn't quite been himself since his discharge, and his friends knew it. They had a good night at the bar, but Shawn had something else on his mind. He almost felt bad for moving so far away from Chloe's resting place as it was routine to visit her grave often. But he found other ways to cope.

****

Shawn began his first unsupervised shift on a warm April Monday. While walking from his car he noticed a figure in a window to his left. About six windows away he could make out a young man, perhaps his own age, looking at Shawn from the West Wing. Shawn waved hello to the man. In return, the man motioned for Shawn, as if to say, "come here". The man's face was emotionless. Shawn ignored this gesture and continued walking.

Upon entering the hospital, he was greeted at the desk by the same nurse that gave him directions to the security office the day of his interview. He learned her name was Riley. She had greeted him almost every day of his training and had once even winked when he passed by. She was beautiful: a young, thin, brown-haired woman, and Shawn was convinced she had a crush on him. He felt a twinge of guilt for being so attracted to her.

"Hi, Mr. Myers" she said flirtingly.

"Please, call me Shawn. I like it better. I went five years by the name Myers and, believe me, those weren't my best days." He said this with a wide smile, showing off his white teeth, courtesy of Air Force Dental.

With a cute giggle, she replied "Okay! So, *Shawn*, a few people and I are going to The Golden Field Cafe for lunch. Want to come? It'll be good for you to meet more of the staff and just relax, you always seem so uptight! I know, I know, the military does that to you. Anyway, you should come."

Shawn gave his best smile. "I don't know Riley. I'd love to but-"

Shawn was interrupted by a scream.

"HELP! THEY NEED HELP! THEY NEED HEEELLLLLPPP!"

Shawn sprinted toward the source, an old woman standing at the end of the hallway waving her cane around while she screamed.

"What's wrong? Who needs help? Where?"

A laugh came from behind the woman, and Shawn bolted up to see a middle-aged white doctor approaching. Shawn stood bewildered as the man grabbed the old woman's shoulders and walked her into the third room away--all the while she kept hollering.

Shawn then realized that it wasn't just the doctor cracking up, but also Riley and the other nurses at the reception desk. Shawn blushed with equal parts embarrassment and confusion. He could hear the doctor in the room quietly speaking to the old woman, who had finally stopped her rant, before he re-emerged into the hallway.

"Sorry for laughing Chief! I'm Dr. Jansen."

He held out a hand that Shawn shook, still confused.
"Uh, hi. I'm-"

"Mr. Myers! Chief of Security. The Army man!"

Shawn was about to speak when Riley came to his side and spoke for him. "That's Air Force man to you! And call him Shawn. He likes that better."

"My apologies, 'Shawn he likes that better'." Shawn laughed more out of courtesy than humor.

"No, don't worry about it. Uh, what just happened?"

"Oh that?" asked Dr. Jansen as he started to laugh again. Even Riley chuckled. "That's Mildred. She's been here longer than I have." He sighed, then continued. "That's just what she does. Take your eyes off of her for more than a minute and there she goes, screaming for help. She's a permanent patient. She fell off of a horse in the early '90s and developed some brain damage. She's selectively mute."

"She sure is loud for a mute person."

"*Selectively* mute, Shawn. It means she *can* talk, she just doesn't," Riley explained. "Nobody really knows why. It usually develops at a young age in children, but I guess she's a different story. Our best guess is that it's a result of head trauma. In fact, her family thought she was completely mute before they brought her here. That cry for help is the only thing she says. It happens every day, I'm surprised you haven't encountered it yet."

"Wow," Shawn said when he could think of nothing better. Nobody said anything after this. Before the silence became awkward, Shawn added: "Well that's my health lesson for today. I better get to my office. I'll see you guys around."

"So, I'll see you at lunch?" asked Riley.

"Yeah, yeah I'll see you at lunch."

****

The following couple of hours were quite uneventful, save for some paperwork, just as Earl had promised. As noon rounded the corner, Shawn leaned back in his seat and flipped open his wallet to reveal a picture of Chloe, worn from all the times he had removed and replaced it. She had made her way into his mind, as she often did, and Shawn sighed. He liked Riley. In his mind, that was not a good thing. When the news came of Chloe's passing, he had pledged his heart to her, silently promising to remain faithful to their marriage despite his widower status.

Doesn't that seem a little ridiculous now? He thought to himself and then felt guilty for even considering it. *What am I thinking? It's just lunch with coworkers, not a date!*

"Hey you!" Shawn nearly jumped out of his skin at the sound, dropping his wallet onto the floor. It was Riley at the doorway. He smiled and stood, reaching a hand to wipe a tear he just noticed was there.

"I'm sorry! Are you okay? Is this a bad time?"

"No, no it's just, uh, allergies."

"It is that time of year... Anyway, are you still up for lunch?"

Shawn bent down to retrieve his wallet. "Yeah, I suppose so."

The pair walked out together and made it to the lot before Shawn realized they were walking alone.

"Where's everyone else?"

"Huh? Oh, they couldn't come. Tyrese got tied up with a patient and Maddison brought her lunch, which is weird. We always go to The Golden Field Cafe on Mondays."

"So, it's just us."

"Yep. If that's okay. I don't want to make you uncomfortable. But I know you've been here since seven o'clock cooped up in that office all day. You've got to be dying for something to eat."

Shawn couldn't help thinking just how beautiful Riley really was. He had never seen her in good light, and she seemed even thinner, athletic even, with a gorgeous smile and picture-perfect teeth. The scrubs she wore seemed like they were made for her, fitting tight to her body. Standing about three inches shorter than Shawn himself made her a tall woman, and if he had to guess her age it would be no older than twenty-three. He shook off the guilt building up.

"I'm starving."

****

They took Riley's Ford Focus after Shawn stated he had no clue as to the route. The Golden Field Cafe was a small family diner in town, and in it the two ate. Riley spoke little about herself, more interested in Shawn's story. In all fairness, he was more interesting. Shawn spoke little about his early life, sparing Riley the boredom, and instead started his story with his military career. He talked about his time stationed in Europe and his tour in Iraq, sparing the details of his wife and her death. Not because he didn't want her to know, rather because it pained him to talk about. Especially to another girl on what had mistakenly become what seemed like a lunch date. He ended it with the moment he first walked in the doors of the hospital, assuming she knew the rest, purposely jumping over the part of the story which he left the military hoping she wouldn't ask. All the while Riley remained as upbeat and flirty as he knew her to be. Shawn made a conscious effort to not reciprocate the flirting, while subconsciously being friendly and not fully turning her away. To the uninformed individual this may have seemed like Shawn was playing hard to get, but in his mind, he just couldn't bring himself to resist her temptation.

Riley's demeanor grew serious. "Shawn, do you believe in ghosts?"

Shawn nearly choked on his food.

"Uh, yeah I suppose I do," he replied, "Do you?"

"Well… I don't know. Have you ever seen one?"

"No."

"Then why do you believe in them?"

Shawn gulped and prepared himself for his answer. "See… I once lost someone very close to me. Before then I never did believe but," he fought back a tear, "after their passing I guess I *wanted* to believe. I wanted to believe in spirits because, well, maybe she was one. And maybe she follows me around. Maybe she's still right next to me. That's why I believe. It just makes me feel a little better knowing her soul is still around me."

"Oh. That's deep. Have you tried to contact them? You know like a seance or a Ouija board or something?"

Shawn shook his head. "See, I wasn't there when she needed me. I'm afraid of what she might say if I did communicate with her. Besides, the only thing I would know to say is that I'm sorry, and if she's a ghost that follows me around, she already knows that."

"That's so sad. Do you mind if I ask who it was?"

Shawn was silent for a moment before lying. "My grandmother. We were really close."

"I'm sorry to hear that, Shawn. I didn't mean to bring anything up. The only reason I ask is because, well, there are a lot of people who believe that our hospital is haunted."

"It's an 'insane asylum' of course it's haunted. Have you ever seen a horror movie?"

She blushed, perhaps a little embarrassed. "Yeah, I guess. But I have to say that it can get pretty spooky at night."

"Have you ever seen a ghost?"

"No. But I had to cover one of Maddison's night shifts one time. And I swear I kept hearing noises from the West Wing. Not footsteps or stairs creaking but, like, screaming and crying. I know that stuff like that isn't uncommon in a hospital, but this was different. I don't know how, but it was. It was only me and a couple of other nurses and Dr. Jansen. I tried to talk to them about it, but they acted like they had no idea what I was talking about. But I swear it's true."

When the bill came, they both reached for it, touching hands for only a second. Their eyes met, and Shawn quickly removed his hand, the check still in it.

"Oh Shawn, let me pay! It was my invitation. Besides you're new. Call it a welcoming gift."

Shawn almost argued that it was the gentleman thing to pay for a meal. But he didn't. *This isn't a date.*

He slowly handed the bill back to Riley, expecting a surprised look that he had given up so easily, but no such look was given. She simply smiled and took it to the counter.

****

The following two weeks yielded nothing out of the ordinary. Warm days kept coming, Mildred kept screaming, and Riley kept flirting. They had gone to The Golden Field Cafe two other times, and she had even come to Shawn's house after a particularly busy day under the guise of returning the office keys he had dropped in the lot. She had been exiting the hospital just behind him when his keys dropped. She tried to yell for his attention but was unable to get it. Shawn was shocked to see her pull into his driveway moments after he did.

"Hey handsome! Hope you don't mind I followed you home, you dropped your keys!"

Shawn stopped at the doorway and took them from her hand and thanked her for bringing them.

"My mom used to say I would lose my head if it wasn't attached. Thanks again, really, I appreciate it."

"Don't mention it," she replied. "I'm sure you would do the same for me."

She took a step back to admire Shawn's home. "Wow! Shawn, you have such a nice house! How many bedrooms is it?"
"Three."

"Oh my. And you live here all alone?"
"Yes."

"I see. I know how it is to come home after a long day like today. To an empty house. Eat dinner alone. It really gets to me sometimes, you know? You ever feel that way?"

Shawn knew the feeling all too but only shrugged in response.

"Well, I'll leave alone," said Riley after a deep breath, hanging her head and playing with the gravel at her feet, "I'll see you in the morning."

As much as Shawn tried to refrain from giving in to her flirty persona, he couldn't help it this time. Inviting her in, at least for a little while, seemed like it was just the right thing to do, even for a man with a dead wife.

"Hey," he said just before Riley got back to her car, "I can't just not invite you in. Why don't you come inside, just for a bit? I'll give you a tour, maybe you can stay for dinner if you'd like."

"Well…," she said with a sarcastic thinking face, "I guess I could stay for a little while." She excitedly hurried to the door, and Shawn let her in.

After a tour of the two bedrooms, he used for a study and for storage, they moved along to the living area, the screened in back porch, the dining room, and lastly the kitchen. It was at this point that Riley asked: "So you aren't going to show me your bedroom?"

Shawn didn't want to explain to Riley that he had pictures of Chloe and other personal items in the room he wasn't sure he wanted her to see. Instead, he decided to make an excuse that something along the lines of the bed was unmade but before he could, she said playfully: "That's alright. Maybe you can show it to me after dinner."

He couldn't be sure if she was genuinely interested in seeing the room or if she meant that sexually, but the latter scared him.

Maybe scared isn't the right word. In fact, he wanted her. Despite his best effort, he just could not resist Riley's charm. She was just so... perfect. It almost felt like his high school days, when he and Chloe had first started seeing each other. In another world Shawn would have pounced at the opportunity to have a relationship with such a fine woman. But these were special circumstances. He had already pledged his heart to another woman, and that is what scared him. He may not be able to fulfill his promise; if Riley tried to sleep with him tonight, he would oblige.

Shawn threw together his mother's recipe for Manicotti. He ate it slowly. He was still playing out what possible scenario might occur after they were done. Riley had removed her blouse and now sat across from him in a white tank top. She stated that it was warm which struck Shawn as odd; he liked to keep it cool in the house.

"That was delicious, Shawn!"

"Well, what can I say, my grandparents are Italian."

Riley giggled loudly at this. They sat for a moment, just smiling at each other.

Suddenly, Riley leaned against the table and played with her hair, revealing at least two inches of cleavage.

"So... about showing me the bedro-" she was interrupted by Shawn's work cell. He was both relieved and frustrated to hear the ringing but answered it, nonetheless.

"Hello," he said into the phone.

"Chief? Chief it's Payne. There's been an emergency at the hospital. It was Mildred. God, she went bat shit crazy! And I don't mean crazy like normal crazy, that's why the old bitch is here in the first place!"

"Well? What's going on? Do I need to come over?"

"Yeah, Chief we're gonna need ya."

Shawn looked at Riley, who seemed disappointed. He pulled the phone away from his ear, pointed at it, and mouthed *It's work. Sorry*. She waved a dismissive hand before getting up to put on her top.

"Alright Payne I'll be there soon. And God damn it, stop calling me Chief. It's just Shawn!"

He hung up the phone and walked Riley to her car. "I'm sorry about this. I still hope you had a pleasant evening."

"I understand," she said, "duty calls."

They stood awkwardly for a few seconds before Riley hugged Shawn around the neck, standing on her tiptoes to do so, and then saying goodbye.

****

Payne was standing outside the main entrance when Shawn pulled in. Payne was a short lanky man of twenty-one years that Shawn didn't much care for. He seemed lazy and rarely shaved his face no matter how patchy his hair came in. He was hired as a security guard just days after Shawn started his new position and seemed a little intimidated by Shawn.

"What's the deal, Payne?"

"Well Chief, uh, I mean Shawn, Mildred. She was screaming 'Help, they need help" over and over! So, when Dr. Andrews went to go talk her down, she stabbed her! The old bag stabbed Dr. Andrews right in the face with a fork from dinner!"

They started to run into the building. "Where's Andrews now?"

"EMS took her as I was calling you. She's at the ER now, I'm sure she'll be fine, but Mildred got her right on the cheek. My God you won't believe the blood."

They rounded the corner into Mildred's room to find her missing.

"Well, where the fuck is she?"

"She took off. She still had the fork and before we could get Dr. Andrews out of the room, she busted her window with her cane and booked it."

Shawn kicked his foot against the bed.

"You expect me to believe a woman who can barely walk jumped out of the window and ran off?"

"We weren't exactly worried about that, Shawn, we had a bleeding doctor to worry about!"

"Alright make sure this mess gets cleaned up. Call in the rest of the security team, ask them to come in. We have to find her."

Only four of the six officers cared enough to roll out of bed to aid in the search. The first evening yielded no results. Shawn knew the woman couldn't have gotten far. She was old and brittle and walked with a cane for, crying out loud. The search during the second evening was composed of local PD and volunteers who had more luck. Shawn received a call Wednesday night not two hours after his chaotic shift. They found her.

Shawn met a Cambria police detective in front of the hospital and explained that Mildred was found in a field just shy of two miles from the hospital. She was discovered at the bottom of a steep hill with a broken neck. The story was that she must have walked the distance, an astonishing feat for a woman in her condition, until she met the steep decline, where she lost for footing and tumbled down like Jack and Jill. It was the detective who made that comparison, laughing while he said it. The detective had likely seen dead bodies before, but Shawn had seen the process. More than once during his time in Iraq had he seen a man take his last breath. Shawn didn't laugh.

****

The following evening, Shawn's day off, Payne called in. Shawn wasn't surprised that all other officers were "unable" to cover, so he took it upon himself. Payne was set to work a night shift, something Shawn had not done yet. He had also never done a routine patrol, outside of the military, of course. His job so far had been just as Earl Fitzpatrick had told him it would be: a lot of schedule making and paperwork. The thought of actually getting to patrol the grounds excited Shawn, he was just beginning to think he couldn't handle sitting at the desk anymore.

He got there at ten that evening and began walking along the East Wing of the hospital. It was storming horribly; a storm like the one that took Chloe.

Walking along he told himself he wouldn't, but he couldn't help stopping when he passed Mildred's room. He looked up and down the hallway to check for any observers before unlocking the door and shutting it behind him. Turning on a flashlight, Shawn scanned the room, not sure what it was he hoped to find. He looked at everything left to right before something caught his eye. A white piece of paper stuck out from the end of a pillowcase. Puzzled, Shawn picked it up. From what he knew, Mildred had lost her fine motor skills years ago.

The chicken-scratch handwriting read: *West Wing needs help, THEY NEED HELP!!*

The paper interested him. He could count on one hand how many times he had gone into the West Wing of the hospital. From what he understood, those patients were the worst of the worst as far as condition. Most of the patients on that side had such severe mental health problems that they were so doped up that they couldn't walk or talk.

But then Shawn remembered what Riley had told him the first day they went to lunch. That she heard screaming and crying. Was it possible that Mildred was hearing the same sounds, all the way in the East Wing? Surely, if an old woman could hear it, it would be loud enough to alert the staff. Unless she was right about the ghosts. This was an old hospital, and surely many patients had died there.

Putting the piece of paper in his pocket, he thought: *Maybe I'll go check it out. After all, it is my duty to investigate.*

He exited the room as stealthily as he entered and made his way toward the West Wing. An older nurse was just walking out of the wing when Shawn approached, and he decided to wait until she was out of sight before he went in.

After walking down the hallway, he immediately realized that this area of the hospital was not kept up as nicely as the rest. Dust covered the floor, and a faint putrid smell filled his nostrils. Sure, this section wasn't visited as often, but it should still be treated the same by maintenance. Shawn had just stepped past the fifth room when the lights flickered. From outside he heard a loud crash of thunder just before the lights went out completely. It only took a few seconds before they came back on, but they were much dimmer now. *Must be the backup generator.*

He kept walking. He could definitely tell what Riley was talking about. Of course, the dim lights had something to do with it, but it was creepy as all hell in that place. Shawn turned a left corner to see a boy around age twelve about twenty feet down the hall. Shawn jumped, startled by this. The boy had long scars all across his stomach and was bleeding from the head. A grown man with a medical uniform painted with blood and a face that was impossible to see in the darkness stepped out from an open door behind the boy and the boy began screaming loudly before charging at Shawn. He turned quickly and fled the way he came, only to run into a middle-aged woman slumped, seemingly dead in a wheelchair. She hadn't been there just moments earlier! Her hair was white, and her eyes were sunken deep into their sockets. Shawn jerked in time to avoid falling directly onto her but tripped over the footrest on the front of her chair and caught himself just before his face met the floor. His flashlight flew from its place on his belt and rolled away from him, but Shawn paid no mind. The woman in the chair began to scream just as the boy was. The screams were so loud!

Shawn kept running. Every room he passed revealed a face at the window, all beating on the glass and screaming: *"Help! We need help!"* except one black man who laughed maniacally while pounding his head on the small window, leaving bloody cracks in the glass. Ahead a hand busted through the glass of a door and caught Shawn by the shirt. Shawn desperately fought to get it free and pulled himself away so hard that his shirt began to rip. The man on the other side of the door released his grip and Shawn fell to the floor. Another rip of thunder crashed, and the lights went out again.

Shawn lay on the ground in a panic. It was pitch black save for the emergency exit signs on either end of the endless hallways. All around Shawn could hardly hear himself think over the roar of cries for help. He could hear the boy he ran from getting closer and this was the motivation he needed to finally get to his feet and run blindly toward the distant red glow. He wasn't even sure he was running in the right direction but was too afraid to run along the wall for fear that he would be caught in another man's grip. Trying his best to run in the center of the hall, the glowing exit sign grew closer, and Shawn knew he was approaching the end.

The lights flickered on, and Shawn had never felt so happy. He bolted out of the hallway doors, passed the reception desk, and out into the parking lot. He stopped only when he got to his car. He couldn't just leave, could he?

He took a moment to catch his breath. He was breathing dangerously hard and could feel every beat of his heart thumping wildly in his chest. He tried his hardest to calm himself and slid against his car until his bottom hit the pavement.

I didn't even run this hard on my last PT test.

"Shawn! Shawn are you okay?" It was Dr. Jansen, running worriedly toward Shawn from inside. He was followed by a nurse Shawn had never met before. Shawn said nothing at first. He wasn't sure what they had seen.

"Sarah said she saw you running like a bat outta hell, right out the door!"

Shawn assumed the worried nurse behind Dr. Jansen was Sarah. "Is everything alright? Now don't tell me you're afraid of the dark."

Shawn forced a fake chuckle. "No, no I'm fine. Just, uh, felt sick. Didn't want to barf on the floor so I ran outside."

What am I supposed to say? That I just saw a ghost? An entire hallway of them? They should have heard that God awful screaming, but they didn't. If they did, they would have done exactly what I just did; ran for their fucking lives. But they didn't. From the looks of it, they were completely oblivious. And my guess it, the same goes for the rest of the night staff.

"I see. Why don't you just take the rest of the night off? You look like shit, man."

Against his own will he said, "No. I can't just leave the hospital with no security."

"It's midnight. Nothing ever happens at these hours."

Shawn laughed. If only. "What about my relief?"

"I'll tell him you had an emergency. He'll understand. We'll keep it on the downlow from the admins. You don't have to, but I would sure recommend it." Grinning, he finished with; "I am a doctor after all. Besides, you're the boss. Who are they going to tell?"

****

Shawn took the doctor's advice and went home. He felt terrible about leaving but could imagine he would feel worse if he had stayed.

The next morning, Shawn texted Riley to ask if she was working. Coincidentally, she wasn't. He asked her to come over.

Within the hour Riley had arrived, dressed in a yellow floral sundress.

"Hi! Is everything okay? When you called you sounded... *off*. Didn't you work overnight? You must be exhausted! What are you doing up?"

Shawn sat on his couch in the living room, and Riley sat next to him, ignoring the recliner adjacent to them in which he expected her to sit.

"Riley please just... let me talk. Something happened last night. In the West Wing."

"Oh my God no. Don't tell me you seen a-"

"Please don't say it. I don't know. But there was something."

Shawn hesitantly recounted the entire story to her. From the note he found in Mildred's room to when he got home. A part of him thought he was stupid for telling this to her, but she remained interested throughout his story and he appreciated it.

"That's so crazy! And you're sure nobody else heard anything?"

"I'm sure. They had no idea what was happening."

Riley sank into the couch cushion. "You know, I used to watch this show when I was younger. About the 'paranormal' or whatever. I don't remember which one. Anyway, I'm sure it was all a load of bull, but I do remember them saying that some spirits just take to people, just like they would if they were alive. Maybe they just think you're special and they want to send their message onto you and the other people who have heard things."

"But why me?" Shawn asked.

"Like I said, special people. I think you're special. I've experienced some things there too, remember? Don't you think I'm special?"

My God, don't start this now, thought one part of him. *Not at a time like this.* The other part of him thought: *You know, she never has gotten to look at the bedroom. Maybe if I show her the bedroom, she'll show me what's under that dress.* The crudeness of the thought physically made him shiver.

"Yeah, but who else has been through this?"

"Honestly, I don't know. We don't rotate days and nights anymore. The night shift is given to basically anyone who wants it. And the people on it now are the freaks who would rather be there at night. It's been the same people on nights for months. And none of them seem to notice it."

Shawn looked out of his window into the yard. "I don't know what to do."

"Maybe you can go to someone for help. Like a psychic medium or something. Maybe she can help make sense of all of this."

The idea seemed ridiculous at first but after some deliberation it seemed like the only option they had. It wouldn't hurt to try it out. After a long search online, Shawn and Riley drove for forty miles to find a medium near Philadelphia by the name of Madame Woodrow. The drive over seemed silly to Shawn, but

Riley seemed rather excited. Which is why Shawn felt bad for asking her to stay in the car.

"What? Why? I want to hear what she has to say."

"Look, she's probably full of shit anyway but… I have some demons, okay? And if on the off chance that she's legit, I don't you to be there when it comes up. Please, just trust me."

Riley slowly leaned over and held Shawn by the face with her small, soft hands. Then kissed Shawn on the cheek. Shawn made an effort not to quiver. It wasn't her fault. She didn't know about Chloe.

"Okay. But when you come back, you're telling me everything. Good luck."

Shawn went inside. He approached an empty table in a small room. It seemed so different from what he had seen in movies. It wasn't a dark purple room with long drapes or even a crystal ball.

"Hello?" he asked.

"Have a seat honey, have a seat."

Shawn still couldn't see Madame Woodrow but he did as she said.

"You have come to see me because you are troubled, right? Something is bothering you deeply, I feel it. Something quite worrisome. A conflict in your mind, am I right?"

Shawn was becoming frustrated that he could hear the voice but not see its owner. He began to stand up when a hand touched his shoulder, guiding him back into his seat.

"Now, now," she said, suddenly standing behind him, "not so fast. Tell me what brings you to see me today."

"Shouldn't you already know that?" Shawn replied.

She looked at him with an annoyed face, one that said "*ha, funny.*

"I'm sorry, I don't mean to be rude. Look, I believe there are some, uh, troubled souls that may need my help. I'm not sure what to do about it because-"

"Give me your hand."

Shawn was taken aback by her request but nonetheless surrendered his hand to her. She held it tightly, running her thumb back and forth across the back of his knuckles. The woman closed her eyes and pointed her nose to the ceiling.

"Why yes, I'm afraid there is a troubled soul."

"*A* troubled soul? As in just one?"

"Yes, it would appear so. A girl. A young girl."

Shawn tried but could not remember a young girl during his encounter.

"She has something she would like to tell you. Would you like to hear it?"

Shawn gulped. His hand was shaking but the medium didn't loosen her grip.

"I-I-I don't know honestly."

"She says your friend is very beautiful."

Shawn froze.

"She says she misses you oh so very much. And she says she hopes you stay as happy as you can be for the rest of your life. 'Love that girl', she says, 'she loves you! Almost as much as I did!'"

Shawn ripped his hand from the woman's grasp. "Chloe? Is that Chloe? Oh my God Chloe, baby, I miss you! Quick, Madame Woodrow, tell her this for me, tell her that I love her so much and I am so sorry for not being there when she was dying." Shawn was screaming now. "I tried to leave Iraq, I really did, but I couldn't, and I just felt so horrible, but I came home as soon as I could, and I visited her grave every single day for weeks! Oh, baby you have no idea how much I miss you!"

Caleb S.

Madame Woodrow was quiet. "Well?" asked Shawn. "Are you telling her?"

"That'll be two hundred dollars."

"What?"

"That will be. Two hundred. Dollars." She said, pronouncing each few syllables as if Shawn spoke English as a second language.

"Are you kidding me? Are you FUCKING kidding me?!" Shawn stood and flipped the table he was sitting at on its top. "Fucking tell her, you old cunt," he shouted through tears, "tell her what I said right now!"

"You think I do this shit for free, asshole? You better get the hell outta here before I call the police!"

Shawn thought better of arguing and stormed out, punching a hole into the drywall as he left. He stopped outside the door and rested against the wall to collect himself before walking back to the vehicle. When he got to the car, Riley asked "Well? What did she say?"

"Nothing. She was a phony; I could tell from the start. Waste of time. Let's go home."

****

They made it back to Shawn's house just before sunset. The two had hardly spoken a word the entire ride home, and when they arrived Shawn silently removed himself from the vehicle and walked up to the door. He had thought long and hard about what Madame Woodrow had relayed to him.

"Mind if I come in, Shawn?" asked Riley. Shawn sighed and let his head fall against the door. "I don't know Riley. I'm pretty tired."

"I think we could both use the company. Besides, you never did show that bedroom of yours."

Shawn didn't respond nor did he look back at her. She continued: "Shawn, look. You were up all day and then worked a night shift. You were tired. Maybe you fell asleep, and it was a dream. A terrible, terrifying dream. Maybe when I told you about some people's belief that the place is haunted, I planted a seed that bloomed in your sleep. Let's just go inside and relax. You deserve it.

Shawn was more than confident that he hadn't been dreaming. But maybe she was right. It was the closest thing he had to a reasonable explanation. He wanted to ask Riley to leave but couldn't muster the courage. Instead, he unlocked the door and opened it wide enough for her to walk in next to him. "You're right, let's go see it."

****

The two went straight to the bedroom and Riley sat on the bed while Shawn spoke about the various objects he had on the shelves and floor. It was pleasing to show someone new his knick knacks and souvenirs. Although she politely nodded and acknowledged what he was saying, Riley seemed a little distracted.

"You're pacing, Shawn, or stalling. Either way, you need a break. You just need to sit down and relax for a while. I know all of this is going on at once, but can you just forget about it for five minutes. Please?"

Shawn sat next to Riley and hesitantly kissed her. It felt good. It had been almost a year and a half since he had kissed a girl. It didn't bother him anymore that that girl wasn't his wife. All he had on his mind was Riley. He had been debating with himself for so long, and he had finally done it. According to Madame Woodrow, it was the right thing. It felt right. Like Chloe had gone away and brought the most beautiful angel God had created and put her in Shawn's path on purpose. That's what Shawn chose to believe.

They kissed for a long time before Shawn recruited the courage to put a hand on her thigh and slowly reach it further up her dress. It took less than two minutes for them to take each other's clothes off and find each other under the covers before they made love.

****

Following the love session, Shawn lit a cigarette, stale as it was likely from the same box he had bought the morning of his interview. The staleness didn't bother him. It's not like he smoked enough to really know the difference. He offered the smoke to Riley, who happily accepted. She took a long drag and coughed the cutest laugh Shawn had ever heard. They giggled and rubbed their noses before hearing the doorbell ring.

Shawn sighed, then gave Riley a kiss before lazily getting up to put on a pair of sweats and going to answer the door. Beyond the door was the detective from Mildred's case.

"Detective, may I help you? Something new with Mildred's case?"

"No, Mr. *Chief of Security*. How do you even call yourself that, huh? How do you sleep at night?" He spat on the ground. "You need to come with me."

"What the hell are you talking about?"

"You heard what I said. You're comin' downtown, let's go."

"No, I'm not going anywhere until I know what the hell is happening!"

Several Cambria police officers appeared from behind the detective and pushed passed, grabbing Shawn by each arm. Shawn didn't resist as they cuffed him and dragged him to the car. No questions were answered on the way to the station. Shawn found himself being led to an interrogation room in the department and was on the brink of tears from his anger and confusion.

After what seemed like an eternity, the detective made his presence in the room.

"Alright, now tell me why I'm here. I haven't done anything! What's the deal?"

"You know damn well what the problem is. You're a damn coward."

"What?!"

"All of those poor defenseless patients were getting their asses kicked by your crooked staff and you didn't do a goddamn thing about it. In fact, you fuckin' ran!"

Shawn couldn't speak. His head was spinning.

"All of those poor patients. The ones in the West Wing of your so-called hospital. We know what you people did to 'em. You drugged them all up so they can hardly think let alone defend themselves. Then your crooked staff raped and tortured every one of them."

Shawn's jaw dropped.

"That's right, the jig is up. We have footage of it too. You know that simple-minded little boy who you met in the hallway? Someone had just knocked his teeth down his throat. All those scars on his body? They whipped him *that* badly. He comes stumbling around the corner and you *ran* from him. Anyway, his mother had been suspecting something fishy was going on for a while so on her last visit she hid a camera in his room. She went back today and got it. She brought it to us, and we watched it, along with all the surveillance footage we could get our hands on from *your* office. You know what was in that footage? You, running down a hall lined with victims begging for your help. Oh, and one of our officers found this in your house."

The detective threw a piece of paper on the table in front of Shawn. It was the note he had found in Mildreds's room that read: *West wing needs help, THEY NEED HELP!!!*

"Sir", Shawn started, "you don't understand. This sounds crazy but... I thought they were ghosts." He felt ashamed for having said this and felt tears forming behind his eyes. "You don't understand. The night I was there, nobody else in the hospital even reacted to the noise! It doesn't make any sense! I swear I never touched anyone! I was honestly scared but when I ran outside, some staff members followed me out to make sure I was okay! They didn't seem like anything was out of the ordinary, I thought I was just going crazy!"

"Are you an idiot? Who do you think tortured and raped all these people? Ever think the other staff members were just trying to save their own skins? You don't get it do you? It was the night shift! All of them! Every night when the last day-shift member left, it was hammering time for these sick freaks. We've already arrested most of them. Dr. Jansen, Sarah Fowler, the lot of them. Now I can't prove that you physically assaulted these patients, yet, but I can clearly prove that you knew all about it and you ran like a roach and didn't do a thing about it. That's enough for me to put you up for a long time."

Shawn couldn't believe what he was hearing. *How could I be this stupid? Have I stooped this low? How can I blatantly see someone in need right before my eyes, and not even know that it's real? Am I insane?*

It took Shawn a moment to realize that this wasn't the first time he wasn't there for someone who needed him.

Chloe would be so disappointed.

Every Day is the Same

Every day is the same. It was the first thing Trevor thought when his alarm went off at 6 am, just as it did the day before and the day before that. As he began waking up, he searched for the other familiar aspects of his morning and checked them off as he found them.

Marissa had all of the blanket pulled to her side of the bed: Check.
The sheet was peeled off of the mattress on the corner by his head: Check.

He was already getting a stress headache from the frustration of another start to a boring, repetitive, mundane life: Double Check.

He swung his legs off of the bed and stood. It was still dark in the room, but he didn't need the light. He was guided by muscle memory from having done this routine hundreds of times. He walked to the closet, expertly predicting how many steps it would take to get there and pulled his uniform out from the darkness. He pulled on his shirt, followed by his pants. He stepped a few feet to the left and felt the bedroom doorknob. He let himself out into the hallway. Only when he quietly shut the door behind him did he finally allow himself some light. He flipped the switch for the hallway light, braced for it, then squinted until his eyes adjusted. He walked down the hall, down the stairs, and into the living room before turning into the kitchen. He found the light switch without looking and steadily began his routine of packing his lunch with yesterday's leftovers, grabbing his route tracker off its charger and a monster from the refrigerator. He did all of these tasks mindlessly and thought jealously of his older brother Chris, who'd been in the military and now worked in civilian law enforcement. Sure, he could be a douchebag, but at least his job was exciting and unpredictable. After slipping on his shoes, he stepped into the small downstairs bathroom and took a piss, then zipped and examined himself in the mirror. His purple and black Fed-Ex uniform was beginning to look a bit bigger on him, or so he told himself. Perhaps a result of all the walking he does on the job.

  He straightened a wrinkle and pinched off some lint, then went back into the kitchen. He heard Marissa's alarm going off just when he knew it would.

He stood with his back against the front door and silently counted down.

5…

4…

3…

2…

Right on cue, Marissa came walking down the stairs.

"You weren't going to say good-bye?" She asked. "You weren't there when I got up. I thought you had already left." It was all he could do not to mouth the words as she spoke them. They had this conversation every morning, but she never seemed to remember.

"Yes, I was" Trevor replied.

"Apparently not." She argued.

"I was!" Trevor said. "I was just waiting for you to come down the stairs." Marissa crossed her arms. "Right. And how did you know I would do that?" "Because" Trevor sighed. "Every day is the same."

After Marissa seemed satisfied with his kisses, Trevor left and drove to work. He took a back road that never had any traffic this early, meaning even his morning drive never varied. He got to the terminals at 6:40 am and watched as his co-workers arrived in turn. Phil, Tony, then Kyler. The four of them walked in together and when Tony clapped him on the back and asked, "How are ya' this morning, Trav?" he put on a well-practiced smile and said, "Livin' the dream, Tony." Tony laughed and clapped Trevor on the back again. "You always say that!"

****

Trevor got his truck loaded and got on the road at 7:00 sharp. He looked through his route tracker and sighed. He supposed he couldn't say every day had the same route or stops but he definitely never only delivered something somewhere once. He was familiar with every house and business he went to from previous stops.

He drove along, passing through town as he predicted everything he would see. It was hard for him to believe so many people lived the same life, doing the same thing day after day. He felt as if he were going crazy and he'd only been doing this job for 2 years. He rounded the corner of East Main and Elm where an old man sat on a bicycle, exactly where he always was at 7:06 am. The man worked at a factory that Trevor would pass later in the day and undoubtedly see 2 middle aged women seated outside smoking cigarettes and gossiping about whatever factory people gossip about. He continued down East Main and stopped at the light. He looked to his left and saw Ms. Little, an attractive grade schoolteacher, sitting behind a window in the East Main Cafe, where she drank coffee before going to work. Seeing her there was usually the highlight of his day. The only thing better was stealing a glance at her ass as she worked out at the gym he delivered to later in the day.

He got bored of predicting the things he would see next and put on some music, though he didn't listen to it. Instead, he reminisced back to a few years ago when he worked in the coal mines. It was hard work, but it was unique. Anyone could be a cop or a mailman. It takes a special kind of man to work endless hours miles underground. He used to feel good, feel used to his potential. He would come home every day tired and filthy but *proud,* bringing home a sense of pride. Now the most he brought home was a sweat stain and depression. The mines had laid him off after fourteen months and he'd somehow let Marissa talk him into getting something "more stable". He knew she was right but hated it nonetheless.

He did his first few stops without issue then sighed as he approached his next one. The dude is a class A retard, always giving drivers trouble. Trevor found his package and sighed again when he noticed it required a signature. On account of the pandemic, FedEx no longer actually required a signature but did require the driver to confirm the recipient was present when the package was delivered.

He took it to the door and knocked. There was no answer, so he knocked again. Still no answer. Trevor dropped the box and filled out the "We missed you!" slip and stuck in the man's mailbox that hung next to the door. Just as he turned to leave, the door opened and a fat, very hairy man stepped out.

"What?" The man demanded. He burped and rubbed his bare stomach. "You trying to steal my box?" Trevor pointed to the insignia on his shirt. "No," he said impatiently, "I'm trying to deliver it."

"Then why are you walking away with it?" Trevor let out a long breath. *Why does stupid shit always happen to me?* "Sir, I knocked on your door twice and you didn't answer."

"Why didn't you just leave it there?" he questioned.

"I'm supposed to make sure you're here first. Why would I knock on your door and then steal your package?"

The man pondered this for a moment, wondering if he should believe it. "Wait, aren't you supposed to leave a note or something if I don't answer?" he finally asked.

"Yes," Trevor replied. "I did. I slipped it into your mailbox."

The man seemed annoyed. "Well, there's your problem! I would have never found that. I don't check the mail; that's a woman's job. My wife does that mail checking." Trevor wanted to say it was probably because his wife paid all the bills, and he didn't have any friends but of course he didn't say anything.

"What is it, anyway?" the man asked.

"How would I know?" Trevor asked, unable to control the bitterness in his voice.

"Well can't you read? What's it say on the box?"

Trevor looked down at it and read what was printed. "Pornfidelity.com 25 of the hottest stars in porn all in 1 collection! Over 200 hours of-" The man waived his hands and motioned for Trevor to stop.

"What the fuck, man?" He asked. "I didn't order that! I have no idea who's that is. Get out of here with that garbage."

Trevor could have argued that it was the man's name and address on the box but decided not to. It wasn't worth it. Besides, the man had shut the door in his face.

Trevor turned and walked back toward the van when he heard a noise.

"Psst!"

He turned and saw the man, this time pressed against the screen of an opened window on the side of the house. "Hey! Hey Fed-Ex guy! Sorry about that! My wife would kill me if she knew I bought that! Do me a favor and leave it behind the porch stairs over there so I can get it when she leaves for work." A woman's voice came from behind him. He turned to listen, then yelled, "Okay honey, be right there!" He turned back to Trevor. "Thanks, man!" The man shut the window and went away.

Trevor put the package behind the steps like the man asked him to, then checked to see if anyone was watching. When he was sure nobody could see, he ripped off the label he had read a minute ago and stuffed it into the mailbox.

****

Back in the van he looked at his watch and realized the interaction had pushed him a few minutes behind schedule. He cursed and wondered why on the rare occasions his mundane routine was interrupted it was because of dumb shit like this.

After an hour of driving a little quicker between stops, Trevor was back on schedule and passed a Casey's gas station. He thought for a moment, then decided all the nonsense with the porno guy and feeling bummed out had earned him another energy drink. He went inside and grabbed a white monster from the cooler and paid for it before returning to his van. Standing by his passenger door was an old lady, approximately 1,000 years old. He was surprised she was alive let alone standing up.

"Excuse me," she screamed even though she was only a few feet away. "Excuse me, young man! Do you work for UPS?"

Trevor tried not to facepalm. "No, ma'am. I work for Fed-Ex."

"My daughter ordered my diapers from Amazon three weeks ago!" She yelled once more. She was very mad, and Trevor worried she may have a heart attack. "I wouldn't know anything about that."

"Amazon told her it would be here in five days! I told her to just go to Wal-Mart, but she insisted they were cheaper on Amazon. Can't you just tell me where they are? Or do I need to speak to your manager! I know you mail people like to steal people's mail!"

Trevor was dumbfounded. *This lady is crazy!*

"Ma'am, I don't know what to tell you. I don't even work for that company!"

"You won't once I've reported you! You should be ashamed of yourself!" She pointed an accusing finger at him before storming off.

Trevor climbed back into his seat and took a moment to understand what had just happened. Earlier in his career this encounter would have been laughable, but after years of retarded conversations like this, it was beginning to get old. "I swear," he said to himself, rubbing his temples in frustration. "From all the bad luck to the stupid customers. Every fucking day is the same."

****

The last of his stops went by mercifully insignificant, although his mood was still soured from the incidents earlier. *At least it's over,* he thought, *just one more stop.* He knew how the rest of the day would go, of course. He would go home, watch TV in his uniform for an hour, eat whatever Marissa made for dinner, beat off in the shower, then watch more TV until 10:00 pm and go back to bed, sleep, and do it all again tomorrow. *Maybe I'll get lucky and never wake up,* he thought.

****

The last of his stops took him into rural farm country. It was beginning to sprinkle and one look at the sky told him there was more in store. It was getting dark despite being only a little after 5:00 pm. It would storm soon, so he made a note to hurry the fuck up before he got caught in it.

A glance at his route tracker told him his last stop was on a country road only a mile ahead. He didn't recognize the address but knew the area well enough to guess where it was.

He turned down the road when he got to it and began his way down a few hundred yards. The cornfield he'd been driving through turned into woods and if not for the mailbox by the road he would have missed the driveway entirely. It was hidden by trees and bushes on either side. He turned left into the driveway and drove for what seemed like forever on the gravel wondering where the hell the house was. He'd delivered a few parcels to a farm further down the road but never even known another house was here. The driveway was about a quarter mile long and eventually opened into a field in desperate need of mowing. Beyond a small yard stood a decrepit but surely once beautiful Victorian home. It was two stories with big picture windows and a wooden wrap around porch. It was impossible to tell what color the original paint had been, for it was nearly completely peeled off and what remained was faded after years of exposure to the elements.

Speaking of the elements, it was really beginning to rain hard now and it seemed to be much darker than it had been only minutes before he turned on the old country road leading here.

This brought Trevor out of his daydream, and he exited the van with the package addressed to the house, which was the only evidence that the house wasn't utterly abandoned as he would have guessed it to be.

The box looked old. It came from a cleaning company called "Squeaky Cleaners!" out of California. The return label suggested it was sent weeks ago. Despite the rain, he stopped just short of the porch, taking in the view of the house up close. It gave him chills to see the huge form like something from a horror movie, its mass of wood and glass (mostly broken), faded paint and crooked window shutters against the ever-darkening sky threatening to release a monsoon at any moment. As if on cue, lightning struck close by, and a cracking thunder followed immediately. *Throw the package down and get out of here,* he told himself. He raced up the steps, half afraid the wood would break beneath him. He got to the top of the steps and bent to set the box on the ground in front of the door when he noticed a spot on the wood. It was about the size of a baseball and impossibly black and seemed to have a fuzzy texture. *Some kind of wood rot or something?* It looked nasty so he moved a few inches to the right and put the box there instead. Despite being under cover, the rain was coming in at an angle and getting him wet anyway. He took a deep breath, bracing himself for the sprint back to the van. He took a deep breath, but just as he was about to book it, a loud slam came from behind him.

    He turned sharply toward the front door. It was closed. He couldn't remember if it had been closed already, as he hadn't looked at it.

    But what else could have slammed? One of the window shutters? Maybe, though he doubted it. *Even if it was, how did it slam?* His heart slowed as he realized what it must have been. *The wind, of course. The wind has been picking up. But was it strong enough to slam the old wooden door?* He decided to stop thinking about it and get the fuck out of there.

He ran to the van and sped away, following the curving gravel driveway until he could see the turn onto the country road that would take him away from here.

Just then, lightning struck again, this time striking a tree at the end of the driveway. The tree exploded halfway to the top and split right in two, the top half falling directly toward the van. Trevor slammed on the brakes just in time to avoid getting crushed but wasn't completely out of the woods. The tree had fallen just in front of him, blocking the end of the driveway. Blocking his way out.

He cursed himself and wished he hadn't stopped to gawk at that damned house for so long. If only he'd left a few seconds earlier, he'd be free. If that fat retard hadn't taken so much of his time earlier, he'd be out of here. If that stupid old lady hadn't stopped him, he'd be at least a minute ahead of time and on his way to the terminal, then home to spend his night with Marissa.

Fuck.

He pulled out his phone and saw exactly what he expected: no signal. There never was any signal in this area.

Double fuck.

He wasn't sure what to do. Perhaps he could walk to the farm he had delivered to in the past. It wasn't very far, but he also knew he wouldn't *get* very far in the storm, which was beginning to produce hail on top of the wind and rain.

He put the van in reverse and carefully made his way backwards to the house. It was hard to see behind him without a rearview mirror but was too afraid of another tree collapsing and landing on his van.

When he got back into the opening near the house, he had all but decided to wait out the storm in the van, then walk to the nearest house.

Unless... he thought, *unless someone is inside this house.* He doubted it, as there were no signs of occupancy. No lights on, broken windows, no vehicles in the drive. *But if nobody is here, who the hell is the package for?*

His thoughts were interrupted as large balls of hail came smashing down. One hit the windshield, followed by another. The third left a small crack, which got a little bigger with the fourth. It would break soon, he knew. Then he would be stuck inside the van as it got drenched inside. Not ideal.

The house, he decided. *I have to get inside.* He would go up and knock. If anyone was there, which he doubted, he would politely ask to seek shelter in the home. If not, he would go inside and stay in the living room until the storm let up. It was old enough to possibly even have a landline telephone he could use. Wishful thinking, but he was desperate.

The large hail drops were few and far between, so he waited for a small break and grabbed a clipboard he found between the seats to use as a shield before jumping out and racing the few short steps toward the door, ignoring the nasty black spot on the wood.

He knocked several loud knocks. No answer came. *Good enough for me,* he thought, then tried the handle. It was locked, but the lock was so old and rusted that parts had chipped away and it was no longer serviceable. With a little pressure the door opened. He wasted no time in rushing inside and shutting it quickly behind him.

Instantly he was relieved to be out of the rain and hail. Next to the door was a stand, on it was a crumbled box of cigarettes, certainly stale, and a vintage zippo. He explored the living room he'd stumbled into, wondering why it was colored so dark. Most Victorians he'd seen were painted colorfully inside. That's when it hit him. It wasn't painted dark. Something dark was on the paint. Something thick and black and furry. Some kind of fungus. He could smell it now. It smelled like death. No wonder someone had ordered some kind of cleaning chemical.

It can't be good to breathe this, Trevor thought. He pulled his work shirt up over his mouth and nose as a kind of filter, not confident that it really helped him any.

The stuff was all over the walls and furniture, but the floor seemed mostly cleared. He considered going back outside and sitting in the van, whether it was busted up by hail or not. Then again, he may never get a chance to explore a house like this again. He would just be careful not to get the stuff on him. He may breathe a little in, which was concerning until he remembered a documentary he'd watched earlier in the year about Chernobyl. People could visit the polluted city for several days before the radiation was strong enough to affect them. Surely if you could breathe in radiation for days, a little musty air wouldn't hurt him. The storm would wear itself out soon enough. *I'll be here for an hour, tops,* he promised himself.

Suddenly he had an idea. He was supposed to wear a mask while delivering parcels. Nobody ever did, of course, but the supervisors were adamant that the drivers at least take one from the box they have in the terminal. Most of the time he just stuffed it in his pocket and forgot about it until he got home and took his pants off. He rummaged in his front pocket and sure enough, he found it. Crumpled up and damp, but he didn't care. It was better than breathing through his shirt. He put it on.

Sure, that he was alone in the house, he explored the room. Everything in it was antique. He couldn't believe it was preserved so well.

The living room ended with an archway with a kitchen on the other side. In it was a table with food still on it, though it was rotting and surrounded by flies. A window was just beyond the table. It was smeared with dirt and grime, but he could see through it well enough. The window faced the backyard, in which he could see a large hole in the yard. It was at least six feet across but impossible to see how deep. To add to the strangeness, there was a thick string of black fuzzy material leading from the house to the hole.

What the fuck is this stuff?

He looked around outside briefly. The sky showed no promise of clearing up. Trevor stayed optimistic. He turned around to face the corner of the kitchen he hadn't yet explored. And gasped.

Slumped in the corner was a body. The body of an old man. Covered from head to toe in the black fuzz. Consumed by it.

"Jesus fucking Christ," he said in a voice barely above a whisper. "I have to get out of here."

Just then, a thud came from down the hallway extending from the kitchen into a part of the house he hadn't been to yet.

"Uhmmmm," something moaned. It wasn't a moan that suggested someone was hurt. It was an aggressive moan. *Like a zombie,* he thought. It was ridiculous but that's what it sounded like.

Fuck this, Trevor thought. He turned back toward the living room and ran to the door. Before he got there a woman crawled out of a room next to the door, cutting him off. Trevor screamed and fell backwards onto his bottom. She wasn't as bad as the old man in the kitchen, but the blackness was taking over, spreading from her arms to her legs. It was just now that he realized she must be naked. Not that he could see anything he shouldn't see under the mysterious material.

"Oohhhkkk," the lady spat, and came toward him. She wasn't really crawling, more like pulling herself along with her arms and dragging her bottom half. Her hair was almost nonexistent, and she had no eyes, only sunken black holes. Either way he couldn't see them.

The door was beyond her. He reared back and kicked the woman, but she barely budged. Instead, she reached out to grab him. He didn't let her touch him. He turned and instinctively ran up the stairs toward the second floor. It was the only way to run besides back into the kitchen, and he didn't think he could stomach seeing the dead old man. Besides, he knew there was no way the woman could get up the stairs without her legs. He came to the top of the stairs and looked timidly around before progressing down the hall he wandered into. There were several doors on each side. They were all closed and for that he was glad. He didn't want to know what was on the other side of any of them. What if there were more people, covered in the black ick, much more capable of getting to him than the old woman.

He could hear the old woman behind him. He turned and saw, to his horror, she was indeed coming up the stairs. Except she wasn't using her legs or even her arms. From her mouth emerged thin tentacles of black string, grabbing and pulling at the stair rail, pulling the woman forward. He turned back around and saw he had nowhere to go.

"In here!" called a voice from down the hall. Trevor turned toward the voice, which came from the last room in the hallway. A girl had poked her head through the crack and motioned for him to go to her. "Come in here, it's safe. Hurry!"

Trevor wasted no time running toward her. He busted through the door and slammed it shut behind him. The girl cowered away from him. He realized she wasn't a little girl at all. She was an adult; she was just so malnourished that she was the size of a child. He could see most of her bones in her face, the rest of her was covered in warm clothes. He couldn't blame her, as it was very cold in there. Cold and dark. It was evening outside, and the clouds absorbed most of the light. There didn't appear to be any electricity in the house. She was wearing sweatpants and a turtleneck but her emaciated face was uncovered. She looked like a skeleton with dark brown eyes. Pale as white paint and chapped lips. She looked like she hadn't eaten in days. He looked around the room and was relieved to see it didn't seem to have spread much to this part of the house.

"What the fuck is going on?" Trevor demanded.

"It's the mold," the woman said. "At least that's what we've been calling it. Don't get it on you."

"What is it?"

"We don't know. All we know is it isn't from Earth. My parents bought the house a few weeks ago and I've been helping them clean it up. Some kind of rock or something fell from the sky a few nights after we started. My dad brought it inside and that's when it started. At first it was just kind of gross, but we didn't think anything of it. The next morning it had spread from the rock to the table it was on. We assumed it was ash or whatever, but it kept spreading. My dad wanted to take it out of town, but my brother had borrowed the truck, and I don't have a car here. It was going to have to wait a few days. We couldn't get any cell service. That's when dad got sick. It affected him the most, probably because he was the only one that held it. Now it's everywhere. It moves slowly but it takes over everything. My mom tried to care for my dad before it killed him and got it all over her too. That's why she's infected. Once it gets on your skin, it spreads so fast. I've managed to avoid it by hiding upstairs. I don't think she can see or hear anything, if she's even alive anymore. I can't tell."

Holy shit, Trevor thought. *Is this for real? Please tell me I'm on Scare Tactics or something.* But it wasn't true, and he knew it.

A high-pitched whine interrupted them. It was a loud sound that seemed to raise and lower in its pitch. He knew what it was instantly. A tornado siren.

"Shit! We need to go downstairs. Can we get out? Is she still outside the door?" Trevor asked. The girl only shrugged. He listened to see if there was noise in the hallway but the storm outside was raging and he couldn't hear anything.

"I'll go check," the girl said. He put a hand on her shoulder. "Don't," he said. "You can't go out there. Let me."   The girl took his hand in hers and smiled. She looked into his eyes. He expected to see those dark brown eyes he'd seen a moment ago. But he had been wrong. Her eyes weren't brown at all. They were black. It was only then that he saw the black mold on her neck beneath her sweater collar and on her arm where the sleeve ended.

Before he could react, the woman's mouth opened, stretching more than humanly possible. She still had his hand in hers. He was just able to jerk it away before her sharp teeth clamped down on them.

"AHAHAHA," she cackled and ran toward him. He wanted to fight her, but knew he couldn't touch her without risking exposure to the black fuzz. He backed away until he felt the wall against his back. The girl hissed an inhuman sound, then charged at him. Trevor reached for the closest object; a lamp on a table beside her bed. He swung it with both hands and connected it to the side of her head. Had he struck anyone else like that, they would surely be knocked out if not dead. The woman was different however, inhaled by the alien material consuming her. She fell to the side but was back up within a few seconds. He took that time to run to the door. He ran into the hallway where the woman's mother was waiting for him. He jumped over her but landed off balance near the top of the stairs and tumbled down them. He came to a stop with his head against the door. He tried to stand but couldn't take the pain in his right ankle. He could tell it was badly sprained if not broken. Luckily, he could reach the knob from where he sat and opened the door. He scooted outside where the tornado siren was much louder, and the porch was drenched in water as it was still pouring rain. He could hear the woman coming pursuing him down the stairs. He knew he couldn't get away. He desperately searched for something to use.

The box he'd come to deliver, the thing that had gotten him into this mess, was next to him. The cardboard was soggy from the rain. He grabbed it and tore at the packaging until he'd uncovered what was within. What he held in his hand was a pump pressure sprayer. He read the label stuck to the front.

Mold Killer.

The woman from upstairs threw the door open and roared a hideous terrifying roar just as Trevor removed the plastic around the trigger of the sprayer. She grabbed him by the ankles and dragged him back into the house. His head hit the doorframe, but he hardly noticed. He had the handle of the pump moving vigorously up and down, building pressure.

She released his legs and mounted him. Her mouth opened unnaturally wide once again. Trevor aimed the sprayer at her and for a terrifying moment didn't think it would work. But after the fluid made its way through the hose it doused her across the face. Its effect was instant. She howled in pain, smoke sizzling off of her face. She removed herself from him, blindly stumbling backwards throughout the house knocking into things and screaming in agony.

Holy shit, it worked!

His celebration did not last long. He was too focused on keeping the sprayer pointed at her that he forgot about the other hideous creature he'd come across initially. The woman's mother. He remembered and turned just in time to avoid being bitten on the shoulder as she crept up on him. He spun around intending to douse her too, but the pressure had run low again, and he would have to repump the sprayer. He cursed and grabbed the handle of the pump. It was in vain however as the effect had apparently worn off and the woman was coming back with a vengeance. He tried to protect himself, but she kicked him with impossible strength, sending him sliding back toward the front door. She held him there and climbed on top of him again. His sprayer had rolled out of reach. His temporary hope of survival was quickly dwindling as she smiled devilishly and spoke.

"Silly man," she spoke, although it was clear the voice wasn't hers. It was deep and horrifyingly masculine, pairing so poorly with the girl's sweet features. "Foolish of you to think you could escape. We've been traveling for hundreds of years to inhabit your poor excuse for a planet. We shan't be stopped by the likes of a depressed mailman. We are too advanced, too smart. Your people are like rats to us. We remember everything and forget nothing."

Just then, the house began to shake violently. The alien being inhabiting the woman seemed confused.

"It seems you've forgotten about one thing!" Trevor cried out. He shoved the woman off him.

"And what might that be?" it asked.

The shaking was growing stronger. Trevor stealthily scooted toward the iron furnace against the wall near him.

"Tornadoes."

The moment the word left his mouth; the roof of the house was ripped away and they were left looking at the sky. The sound was incredible, like he was underneath a moving train. A huge funnel cloud was over them, sucking up the house and everything in it. The iron furnace, however, was built into the foundation beneath the home. It didn't budge.

Caleb S.

Trevor used all of his strength holding onto the bars of the furnace while he watched the woman soar into the air and get jerked around in circles by the currents of the wind. The spray bottle had rolled closer to him now and he trapped it with his foot before it too could be taken in the air. All the rattling had knocked off the pack of cigarettes and the zippo lighter placed on the stand near the door, and it was just in reach. With an arm wrapped through the bars of the furnace, Trevor pumped the sprayer until it wouldn't pump anymore. He took the vintage zippo and was certain it wouldn't work. However, on the first flick of the flint it came alive with man's first invention.

He held the flame in front of the sprayer barrel and pulled the trigger, sending a stream of flames into the air, swirling around inside the funnel catching itself on the old dry furniture and age-old wood. Before he knew it the entire tornado was a towering ball of fire, blazing and consuming as it tore through the house.

Just when Trevor thought he could hold on no longer, the wind let up. The tornado began to dissipate and make its way back into the sky. Things were falling all over the land, and he was lucky nothing struck him on its way down. It wouldn't matter, however, as most of it had burned up in the fire. All that was left of the house was the brick foundation and the furnace he clung to. All the black alien mold seemed to have been killed in the fire.

There was one other thing left.

His van.

Unbelievably, his van sat in the driveway just as it had earlier. It was covered in ashes and debris but seemed otherwise unharmed. He let go of the furnace and knew he would have a nasty bruise there later. He didn't care about that.

****

Trevor drove straight home. The storm had cleared completely. He was prepared to drive the van over grass or bushes if he needed to but as luck would have it, the tornado had apparently moved the fallen tree off of the driveway. His leg still hurt like hell, but he managed to ignore it for the most part. He didn't bother returning the van to the terminal. When he came into town his phone exploded with messages from his boss wondering where the hell he was. He ignored them. Just as he got home, a call came from the office. He answered but simply said, "Leave me alone. I quit. I'm Fed-Up with Fed-Ex." then hung up.

The business at the house, though it felt like days had gone by, had realistically only taken a little over an hour, which was roughly the same amount of time it would have taken for Trevor to drive to the terminal from the house and drive his own car home. This meant that Marissa would assume he was home and done for the night, unless she saw the van outside, but he knew she wouldn't.

He got out and searched himself very carefully, making sure none of the alien mold had gotten onto him. He found none. He looked in the side mirror and straightened himself out. He had some blood on his face that he wiped away. His hair was crazy, and he was soaked but he would just tell her he had been caught in the rain.

He limped to the front door and still worried he would track something inside. They lived in town, so he was careful to make sure no one would see him when he stripped to his underwear outside before going in.

He opened the door to the smell of baking meat. Marissa was at the stove, just where she always was when he got home from work. She saw him and gasped audibly. "What the hell are you doing? Why are you naked?"

"I'm soaked," Trevor explained. "My clothes are gross. I didn't want to bring any mud into the house. I'll get them later." Except he knew he wouldn't. He would leave them there until the middle of the night, then carefully move them to the backyard, where he would burn them just to be safe.

"Well go take a warm shower before you get sick. Dinner will be done shortly."

He decided a shower sounded wonderful. He gave her a kiss, then went into the bathroom. He showered quickly and got out, dressed in some comfortable pajamas, and sat at the table where Marissa was making his plate. He didn't think he was hungry but when the first bite touched his stomach, he couldn't stop. He devoured his food and wasted no time making himself more. After dinner, they snuggled on the couch for a movie. It was a wonderful night spent like all the others, and he relished its familiarity. When Trevor suggested going to bed early, Marissa agreed. They walked upstairs together and climbed into bed.

"Goodnight," Marissa said as she pulled the covers to her side of the bed. She heard no answer. Trevor was already asleep.

****

Trevor dreamed he was still in the house. It hadn't been destroyed by a fire tornado. The woman had gotten to him before he could spray and she'd bitten his face, tearing it off and chewing with her mouth open unnaturally large. "I'm not done with you yet," the monstrous woman said to him. Wiry black tentacles erupted out of her eye sockets, plunging into his mouth and nose. He could feel them extending in every direction. Tearing down his throat into his stomach. Crushing through his sinuses into his brain. He could feel the evil moving in him. Feel death taking over…

****

He woke up at 6 am, just as he did every day. They hadn't bothered to shut the curtain the evening before, and a trickle of early morning sunlight was streaming into the room. His heart began to slow as he realized it had all only been a dream.

He snuggled close to Marissa and hugged her tight. She wrapped an arm around his and squeezed a loving embrace. He felt a strong feeling of intimacy. Until the blanket slid down her arm, exposing her wrist. Trevor's heart sank. He felt like throwing up.

"Marissa?" he asked in a hoarse whisper.

"Hm?" she asked, still mostly asleep.

"What's this on your arm?" He prayed it wasn't what he thought it was. Maybe it was a smear of makeup or a piece of food from last night.

Please God let it be anything else but that.

"I don't know," she said. "I brought your clothes in from outside while you were showering last night and put them in the washer for you. Your shoes had black shit all over them. I got a little bit on my hand and couldn't wash it off. I'll try again later."

Trevor thought back to when he kicked the old lady. He hadn't wondered if any mold had gotten onto him and hadn't thought to check the bottom of his shoes when he got undressed. Marissa said it was only "a little bit" but it was not. It may have been at first, but now it was all across her arm starting from her wrist and ending just beneath her shoulder. He remembered the words from the woman in the house.

Once it gets on your skin, it spreads so fast…

He wouldn't tell her. Not right now, anyway. Not today, if he could help it. *No,* he decided, *I want today to be just like every other day.*

Caleb S.

Author's Note

We Are Not Alone. My print debut (mostly; *They Need Help* was previously published in a horror anthology that nobody bought a few years back). Not long ago, I had a serious conversation with myself in which I all but decided to give up on writing. I didn't have much confidence in my writing talent or ability to dedicate the time. After experiencing some life-changing events in the summer of 2024 and the encouragement of my beautiful wife, I decided to say, "fuck it". I may be a full-time employee for the state of Illinois, a father to a bunch of crazy toddlers, and a grad student; what's one more thing? I rediscovered my love for reading and writing, started a writing group with some friends, and created within myself an undeniable urge to see my name on a book. This collection is a sort of grab bag of stories I had already completed over the last few years. I don't necessarily believe that they showcase my writing ability to its fullest potential, as they were written prior to my decision to pursue writing more seriously. I never expected them to be seen by anyone other than my closest friends. However, I have to say I am still proud to release them and save my longer, more serious works for the future.

Rose is perhaps the deepest of these stories. It was based on the very real fear of losing the woman I love.

Chatty Cathy was written originally as a prologue for my first novel attempt that I ultimately decided was strong enough to stand on its own.

We Are Not Alone was one of the stories I wrote for my writing group. If it isn't obvious from the title of this collection, it is clearly my favorite among these stories.

The Diggins was another writing club story, although I had been brewing the idea for months before that. I liked the idea of a lonely young boy, such as I was, seeking companionship from beyond the grave.

They Need Help is the oldest of these stories. I wrote this in the summer of 2018 for a writing class I participated in. It was published as part of an anthology titled *Wicked Writings* that, as I said, was less than successful, and I didn't want it to go to waste.

Every Day is the Same is an interesting one. Alien-zombie things fought off by a Fed-Ex driver and taken down by a fire tornado? What a concept. I wrote this story as a gift for my younger brother on his birthday. He's a boring fella, sorry to say, working as a Fed-Ex delivery driver at the time. This was a tradition I carried on for a few years, and perhaps another of those birthday stories will see the light of day in another collection. It follows two brothers who visit a bed and breakfast in Oregon and find themselves in the grasp of a deadly cult populated entirely by goth women. It's over the top, ridiculously gory, and a little funny. Sound interesting? Stay tuned for it.

If you made it this far, I appreciate you for reading. Until next time.

Osculum obscenum

-Caleb S.

April 1, 2025

About the Author

    Caleb S. is an author from southern Illinois. He is an Air Force veteran, a proud husband, and father to five. He enjoys drumming, combat sports, and writing. After being kicked out of his rock band and getting beat up too many times, there was only one option left. *We Are Not Alone* is his debut publication of short horror fiction.

Caleb S.

Made in the USA
Monee, IL
30 May 2025